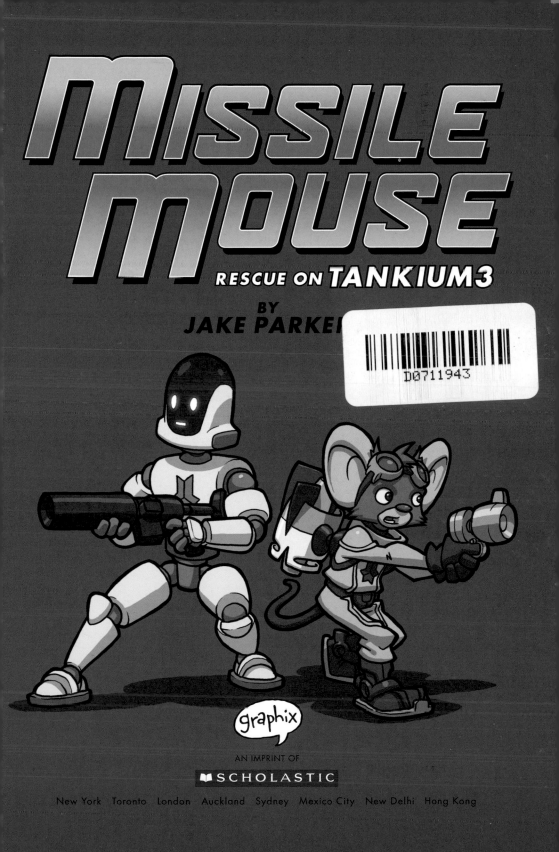

MISSILE MOUSE

RESCUE ON TANKIUM3

BY
JAKE PARKER

graphix

AN IMPRINT OF
SCHOLASTIC

New York Toronto London Auckland Sydney Mexico City New Delhi Hong Kong

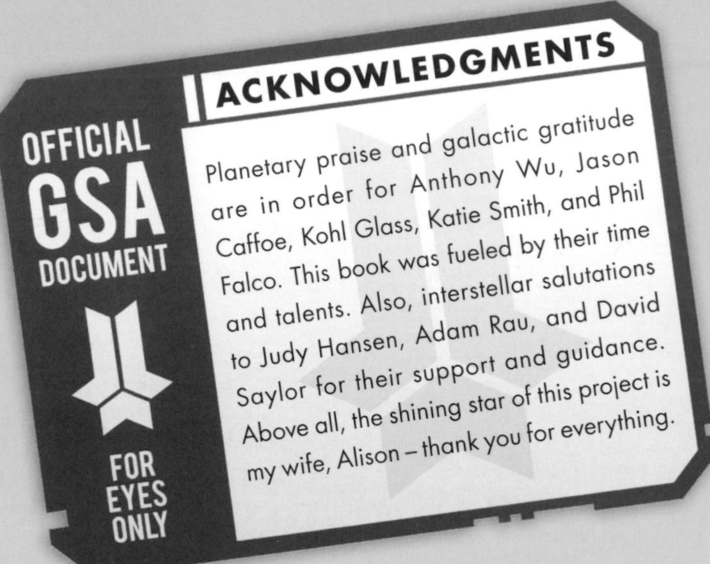
ACKNOWLEDGMENTS
OFFICIAL
GSA
DOCUMENT
FOR
EYES
ONLY
Planetary praise and galactic gratitude are in order for Anthony Wu, Jason Caffoe, Kohl Glass, Katie Smith, and Phil Falco. This book was fueled by their time and talents. Also, interstellar salutations to Judy Hansen, Adam Rau, and David Saylor for their support and guidance. Above all, the shining star of this project is my wife, Alison – thank you for everything.

ISBN 978-0-545-11716-6 (hardcover)
ISBN 978-0-545-11717-3 (paperback)

Library of Congress Cataloging-in-Publication Data Available

10 9 8 7 6 5 4 3 12 13 14 15

First edition, January 2011
Edited by Adam Rau
Creative Director: David Saylor
Book design by Phil Falco
Printed in Singapore 46

VENTURI,
CAPITAL PLANET OF
THE GALACTIC UNION.

huf
huf

FREEZE, OR I BLAST YOU!

I SAID FREEZE!!
LOOK OUT!

THIS GUY IS NUTS!

FWOOSH

THUNK

SHOOOM

THUD!!

Huf
Huf

GET OFF MY ROOF, YA DOOFUS!!

BRAKE!

SCREEECH!

GONE!

Huf
Huf

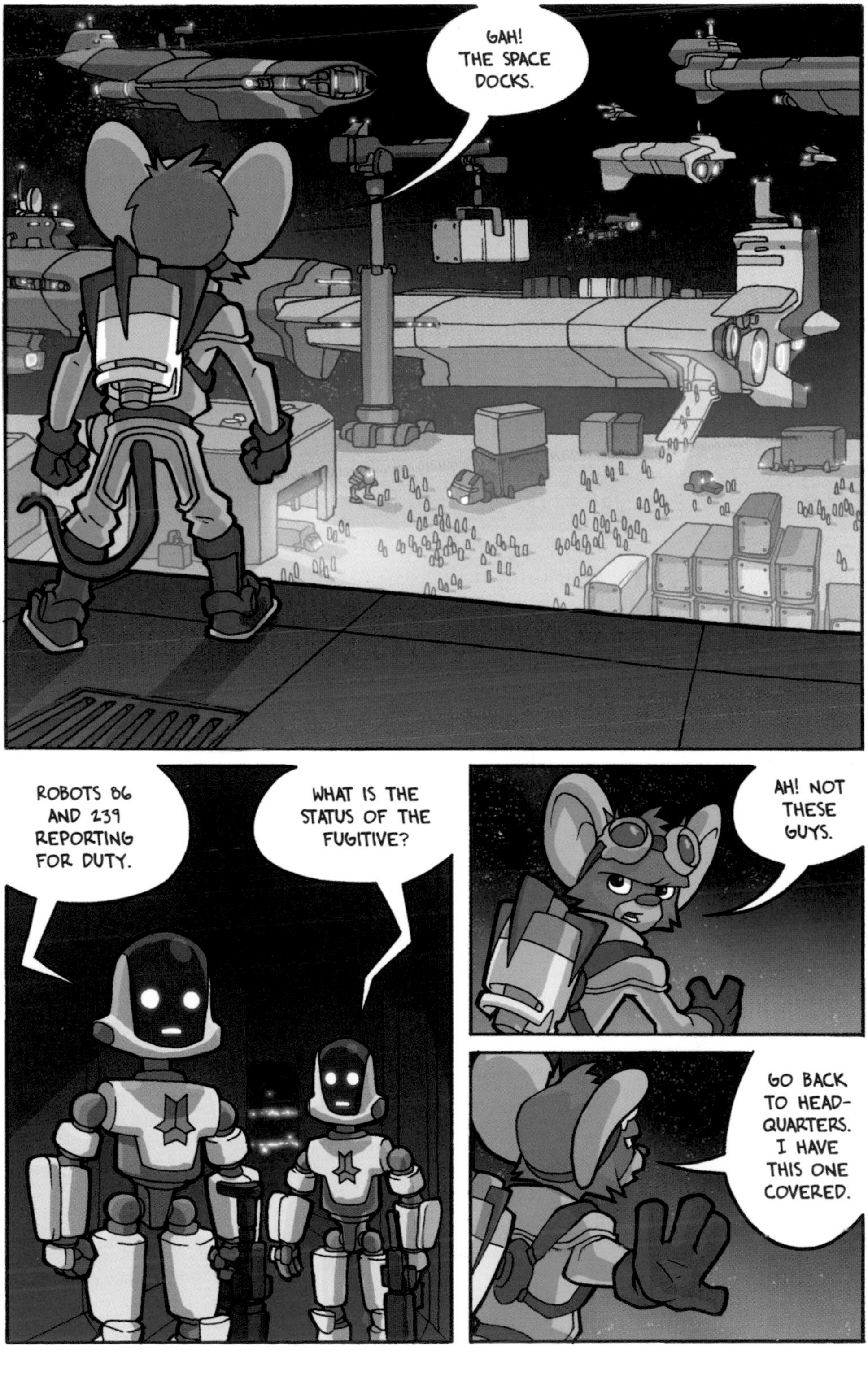

GAH! THE SPACE DOCKS.

ROBOTS 86 AND 239 REPORTING FOR DUTY.
WHAT IS THE STATUS OF THE FUGITIVE?

AH! NOT THESE GUYS.

GO BACK TO HEAD-QUARTERS. I HAVE THIS ONE COVERED.

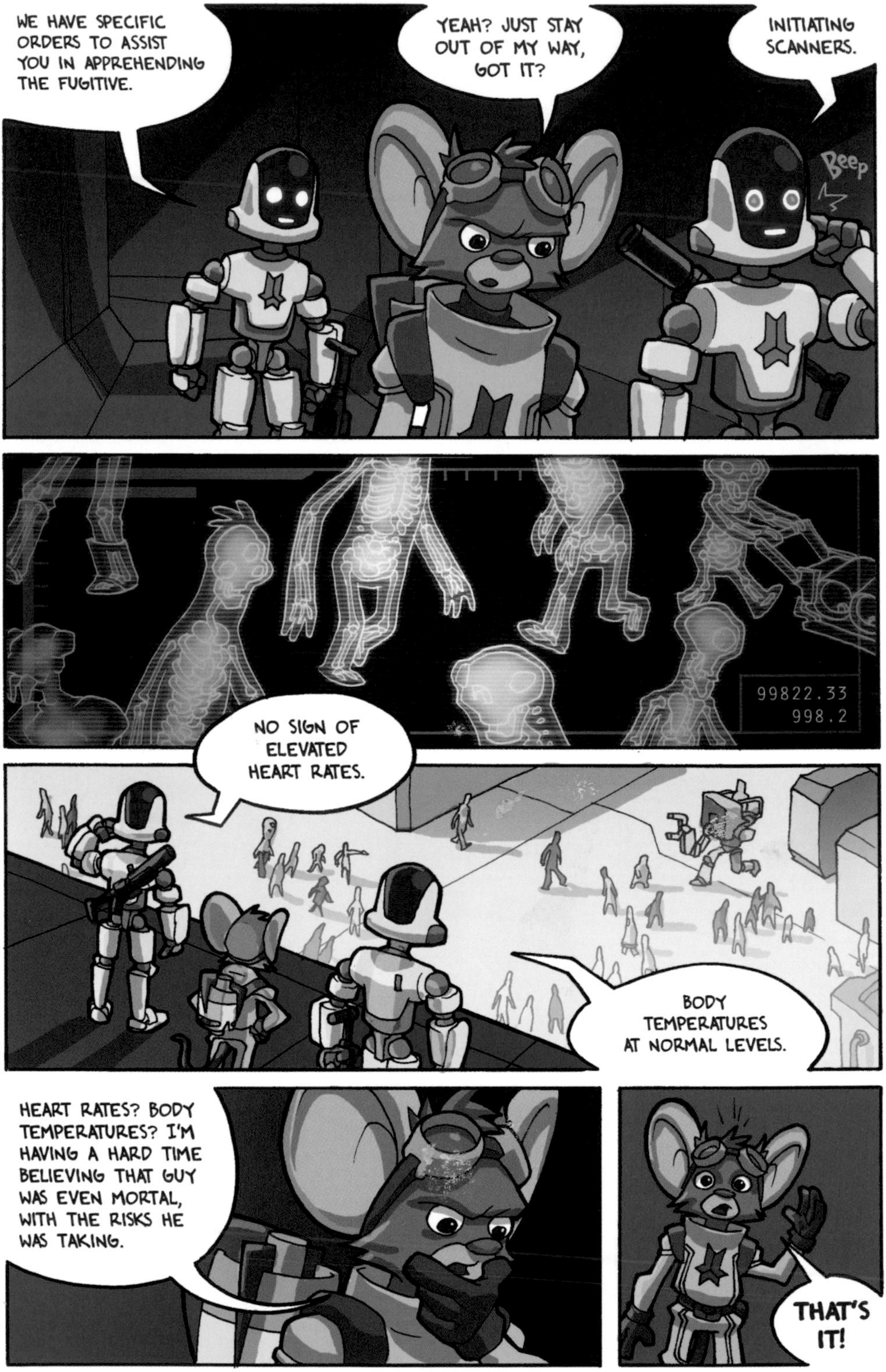

99822.33
998.2

NO SIGN OF ELEVATED HEART RATES.

BODY TEMPERATURES AT NORMAL LEVELS.

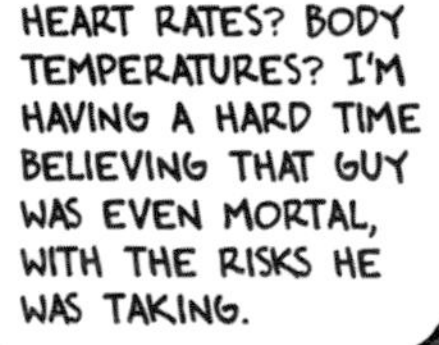

COSMIC-COLA
7

CHACK!
Beep

PLUNK!

BOOM

FREE COSMIC-COLA!

OUTTA MY WAY!
MINE!
MOVE IT!
FREE!
COSMIC-COLA!
HANDS OFF!
FREE!
FREE!

WHERE DID HE GO??

THERE YOU ARE.

FUGITIVE DETECTED.
ENGAGE SUSPECT?
AFFIRMATIVE.

SPLASH

SPLOOSH!

POOMPH!

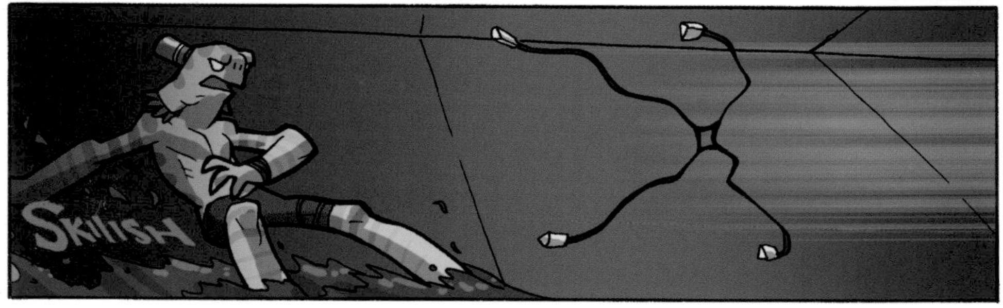
SKIIISH

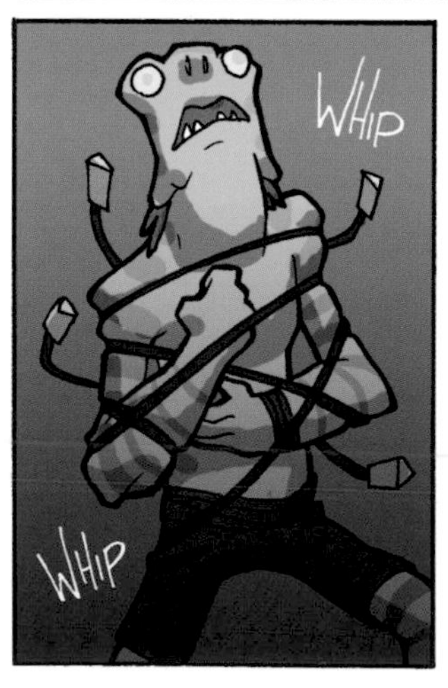
WHIP
WHIP

EXCELLENT WORK, 239.

WHAT PART OF "STAY OUT OF MY WAY" DO YOU BOTS NOT UNDERSTAND?

YOU DO NOT HAVE SUFFICIENT PRIVILEGES TO COUNTERMAND OUR ORDERS.

YEAH? WELL, YOU BOTS DON'T HAVE SUFFICIENT FIELD EXPERIENCE TO HANDLE THIS TYPE OF WORK.
CASE IN POINT, YOUR WEAPONS AREN'T IN A READY POSITION.

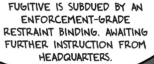

FUGITIVE IS SUBDUED BY AN ENFORCEMENT-GRADE RESTRAINT BINDING. AWAITING FURTHER INSTRUCTION FROM HEADQUARTERS.

WHAT IS *THAT* THING? YOU GUYS SCAN IT YET?

DO NOT UNDERSTAND "THING." PLEASE SPECIFY WHAT IT IS YOU SPEAK OF.

WHEN YOU SEE A LARGE METAL OBJECT STICKING OUT OF SOMEBODY'S HEAD, IT'S A GOOD SIGN SOMETHING ISN'T RIGHT WITH HIM.

ZZZZOT

GRAK!

AAAAH!!

WH-WHERE AM I?!! WHAT ARE YOU GUYS?! AAAH!! WHERE IS THIS?!!
HOLD HIM DOWN, 239!

?

THIS IS SOME KIND OF MIND CONTROL DEVICE! HE HAS NO IDEA WHAT HE'S BEEN DOING!
LET ME GO!
WHAT DO YOU WANT?!
WHERE'S MY FAMILY?!
BY ORDER OF THE GALACTIC SECURITY AGENCY, STAND DOWN, FUGITIVE!

YOU GUYS LET GO OF HIM! YOU'RE SCARING HIM!

GARRRR

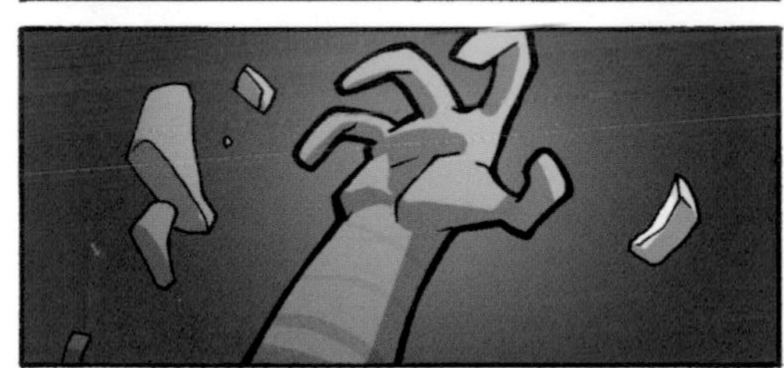

SMASH

Huf
Huf
Huf
S-S-TTAND... D-D-DOWN, FUGITI-I-IVE!

Grrr
EASY, EASY. I'M NOT GOING TO HURT YOU.

Sploosh
Sploosh
Sploosh

PIECE-OF -JUNK ROBOTS.

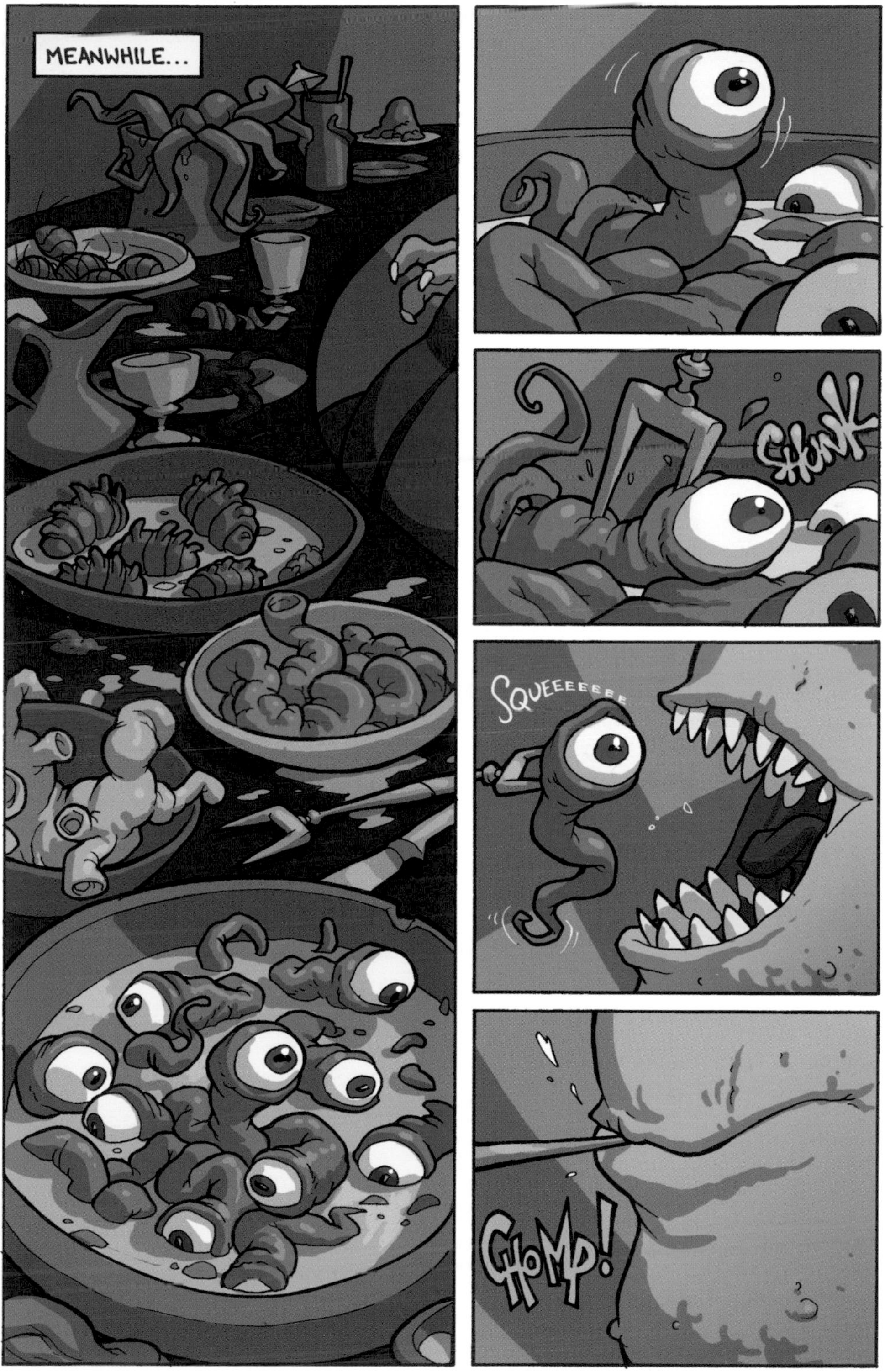

MEANWHILE...

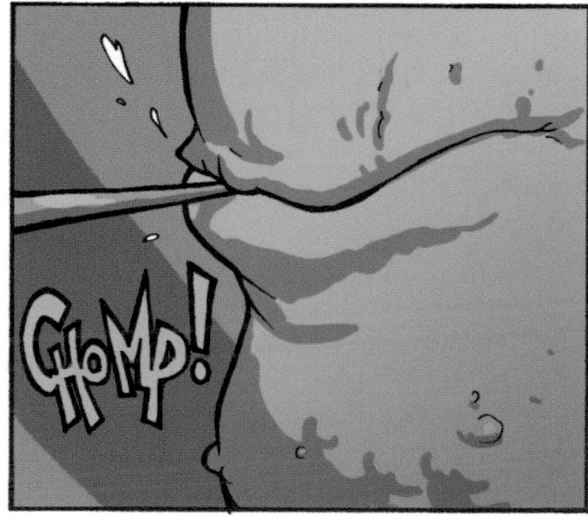

EX-EXCUSE ME... KING BOGNARSH? I HAVE AN-AN URGENT M-MATTER.
THE GAGWARTS ARE DELICIOUS TONIGHT!
TELL THE CHEF I'LL HALT HIS TORTURE FOR THE NEXT THREE DAYS.

VERY M-MERCIFUL OF YOU. BUT, S-SIR...IF I MAY, WE HAVE A P-PROBLEM.

GO ON! WHAT IS IT?!

ONE OF THE SLAVES HAS GONE OFF-LINE AND THE DELIVERY ON VENTURI WAS A FAILURE.

WHAT?!!

THE GSA FOUND OUT THAT OUR TRANSPORT SHIP EVADED THE VENTURI CHECKPOINTS AND THEY SENT MISSILE MOUSE TO INVESTIGATE!

MISSILE MOUSE!!

KONK!

WHO DO WE HAVE ON VENTURI WHO CAN CLEAN UP THIS MESS?
LET'S SEE...

WELL, WE HAVE A FEW OPTIONS...
THERE'S TRAGUS.
NAH, I OWE HIM MONEY.

HOW ABOUT RETINOID?
TOO DOPEY.

GASTROPODAR?
TOO SLOW.

MANDILACK?
HE'S A HACK.

BLAZING BAT?
BLAZING BAT...

YES...YES!
I LIKE THAT BAT, VERY PROFESSIONAL.

TELL HIM I WANT THE SLAVE HUNTED DOWN AND ELIMINATED, AND I WANT ALL EVIDENCE OF MY SHIPMENT DESTROYED.
ANYTHING ELSE, SIR?

AND I WANT MISSILE MOUSE'S HEAD ON MY WALL!

YES, SIR!

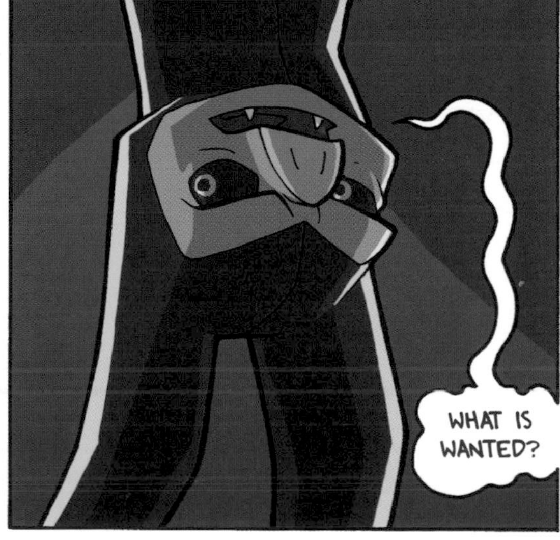

THE VENTURI SEWER SYSTEM.
SPLISH
SPLOOSH

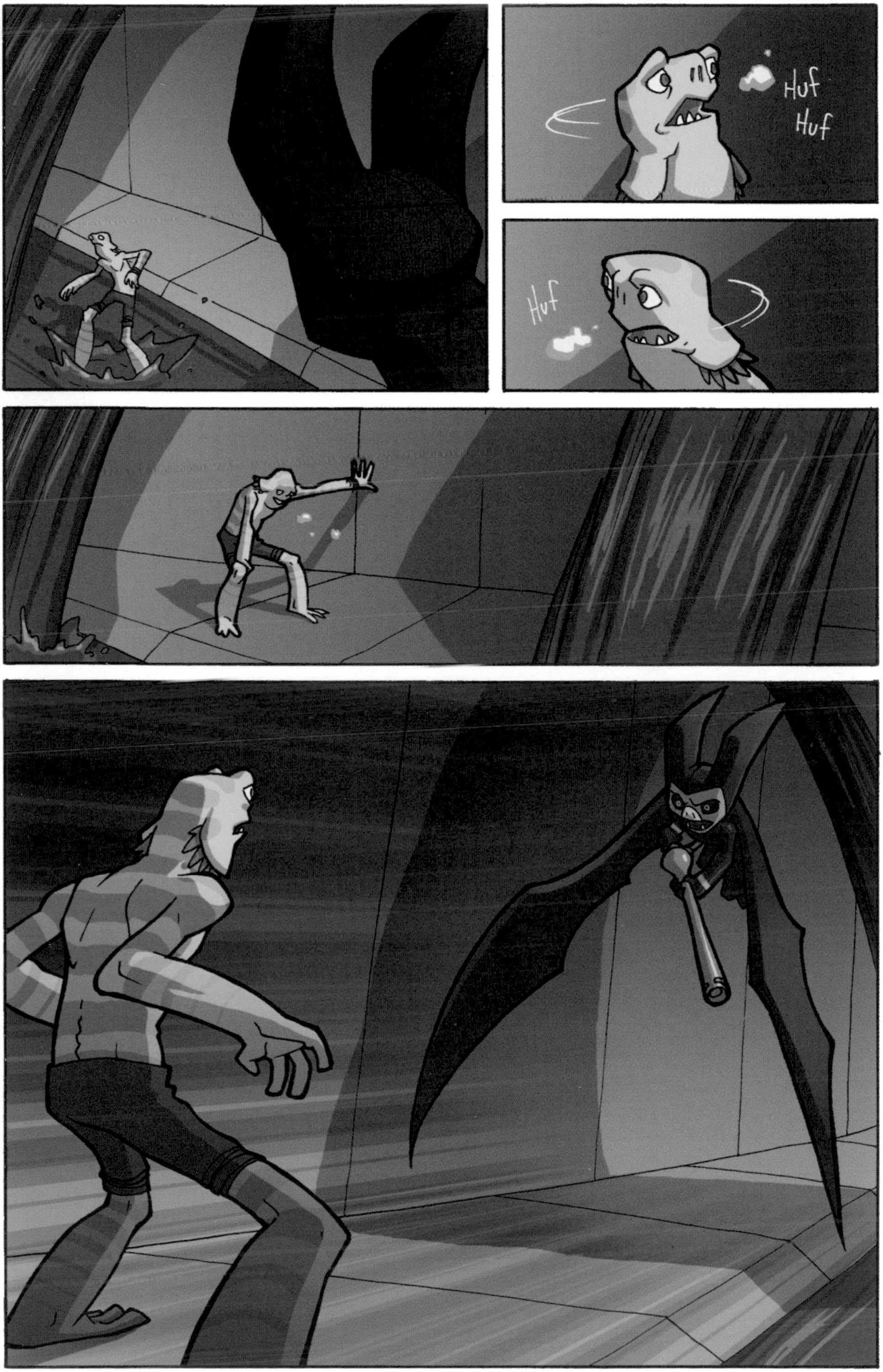

Huf
Huf

Huf

FWASHHH!

BLAST
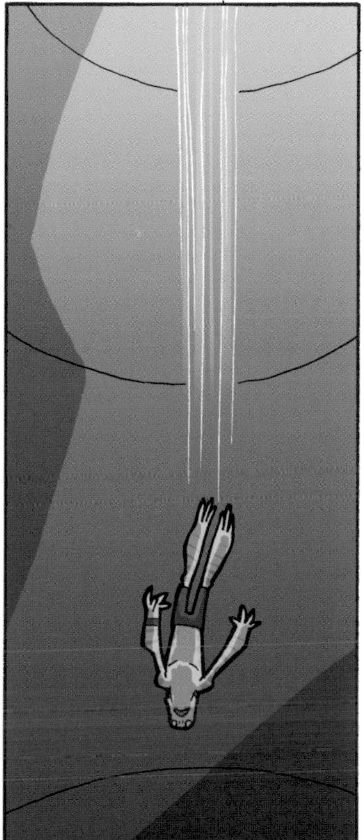

SNAG!

!

GET BACK!

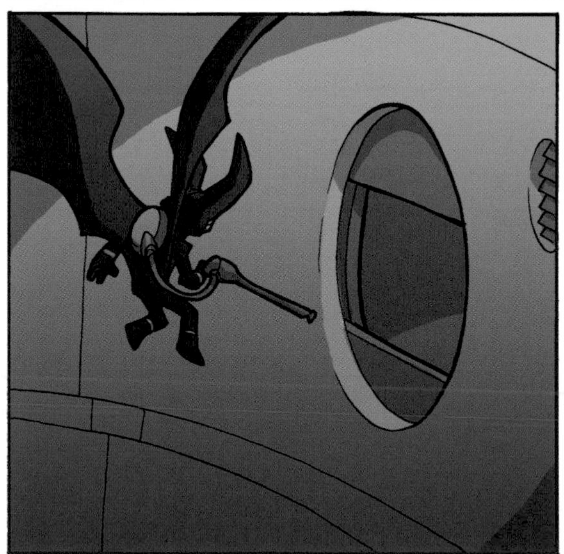

CRANK!

CLANK!

FWOOSHH

RUN! RUN!

THIS IS MISSILE MOUSE. I NEED A TRANSPORT AT EXTRACTION POINT 33-B RIGHT NOW!

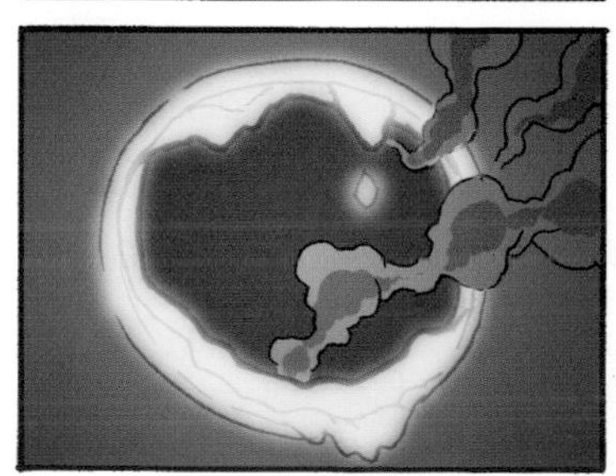

LOOKS CLEAR.

ARE YOU ALL RIGHT?
I'M FINE. THANK YOU.

I'M AGENT MISSILE MOUSE. I'M HERE TO HELP YOU.

YOU SAVED MY LIFE. THANK YOU.

MY NAME IS LASUKUS,
AND I WANT TO GO HOME.

I CAN HELP YOU GET THERE, BUT FIRST MY FRIENDS ARE GOING TO WANT TO ASK YOU SOME QUESTIONS.

WE'RE ON. GO! GO!

THAT BLASTED RODENT!

THAT NIGHT,
GSA REPAIR GARAGE.
GSA ROBOTICS

LIGHTS ON. GOOD, HE'S HERE.

BITNER?

BITNER?!
HEADS

THERE YOU ARE.

HEY, BITNER, YOU HEAR ME?!
DO BE DOO DO BA DAAA!

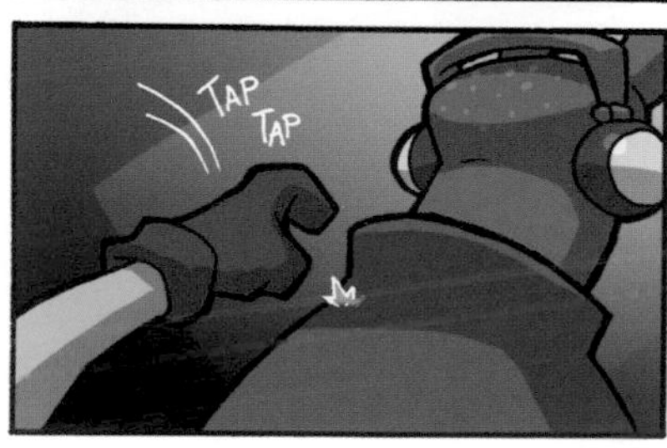
TAP TAP

GAH!

EASY, BITNER! IT'S ME!!

OH, MISSILE MOUSE! YOU SCARED THE DICKENS OUT OF ME.

SO WHAT'S UP? BEEN OUT SAVING THE GALAXY AGAIN?

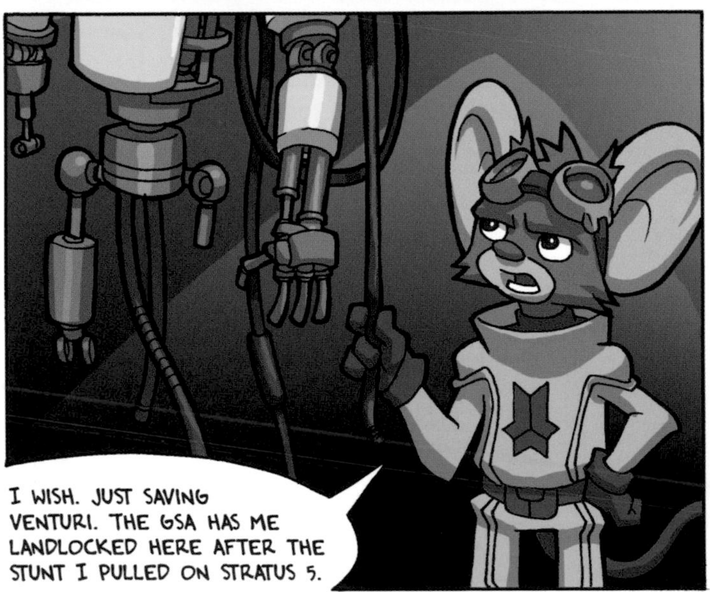
I WISH. JUST SAVING VENTURI. THE GSA HAS ME LANDLOCKED HERE AFTER THE STUNT I PULLED ON STRATUS 5.

I HEARD ABOUT THAT. YOU'RE LUCKY YOU MADE IT OUT IN ONE PIECE.

YEAH, WELL, IT LOOKS LIKE THESE GUYS AREN'T AS LUCKY.

VENTURI IS TOUGH ON THESE GUYS, BUT THEY DO GOOD WORK.

I'D STILL RATHER HAVE SOMETHING WITH A CONSCIENCE OUT THERE ON THE STREETS.

HEADS
HEARTS
LEGS
THESE BOTS MAY DO A GOOD JOB, BUT IN A TIGHT SITUATION THERE'S NO SUBSTITUTE FOR QUALITY GRAY MATTER AND A BEATING HEART.

TRUE, BUT YOU KNOW THE GSA IS STRAPPED FOR GOOD AGENTS...FOR PLUTO'S SAKE, THEY HIRED YOU!

VERY FUNNY, BITNER.

SERIOUSLY, THOUGH, EVERY HIT ONE OF THESE BOTS TAKES OUT THERE IN THE FIELD LETS YOU KEEP DOING YOUR JOB THAT MUCH LONGER.

TAKE NUMBER 44 HERE.
HE'S ONE OF OUR FINEST SECURITY BOTS. SEEN MORE ACTION THAN SOME AGENTS.

JUST YESTERDAY HE WAS AMBUSHED BY A RIP SQUAD WHILE INVESTIGATING A SECURITY BREACH IN THE INDUSTRIAL DISTRICT.

I'LL JUST SWITCH OUT HIS ARMS HERE...

INSTALL A NEW TEMPERATURE ALTERNATOR THERE, AND HE'LL BE RIGHT BACK ON THE JOB.

IF AGENTS WENT THROUGH WHAT HE JUST DID, THEY'D BE OUT OF COMMISSION FOR MONTHS. THAT IS, IF THEY SURVIVED.

ANYWAY, WHAT BRINGS YOU HERE, MISSILE MOUSE?

THIS. WE FOUND IT ATTACHED TO THE HEAD OF A GUY WE JUST APPREHENDED.

HE HAS NO MEMORY OF THE ENTIRE LAST WEEK. IT'S A COMPLETE BLANK.

FASCINATING! I HAVEN'T SEEN ONE OF THESE IN A LONG TIME.

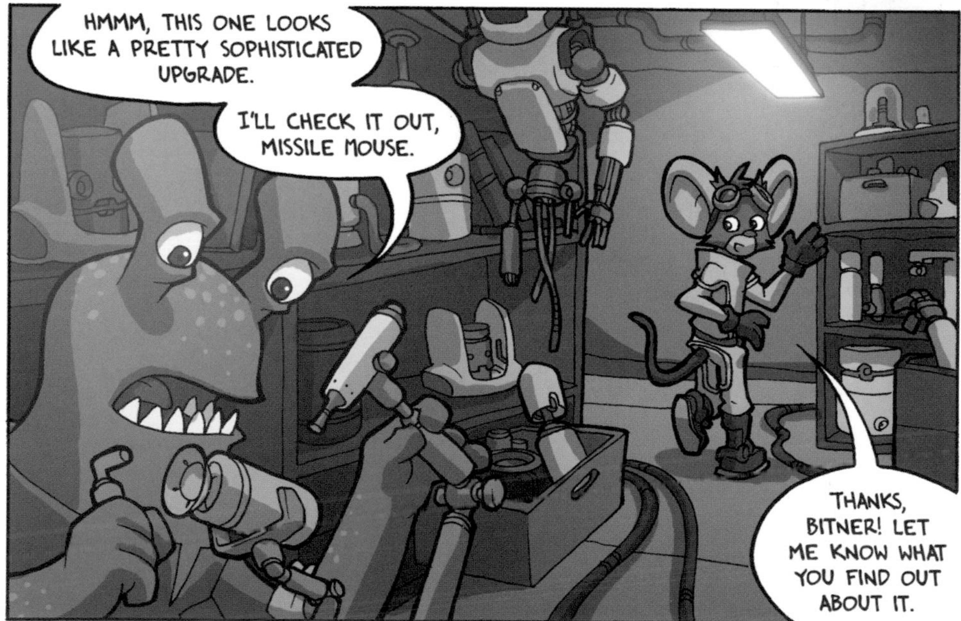
HMMM, THIS ONE LOOKS LIKE A PRETTY SOPHISTICATED UPGRADE.
I'LL CHECK IT OUT, MISSILE MOUSE.
THANKS, BITNER! LET ME KNOW WHAT YOU FIND OUT ABOUT IT.

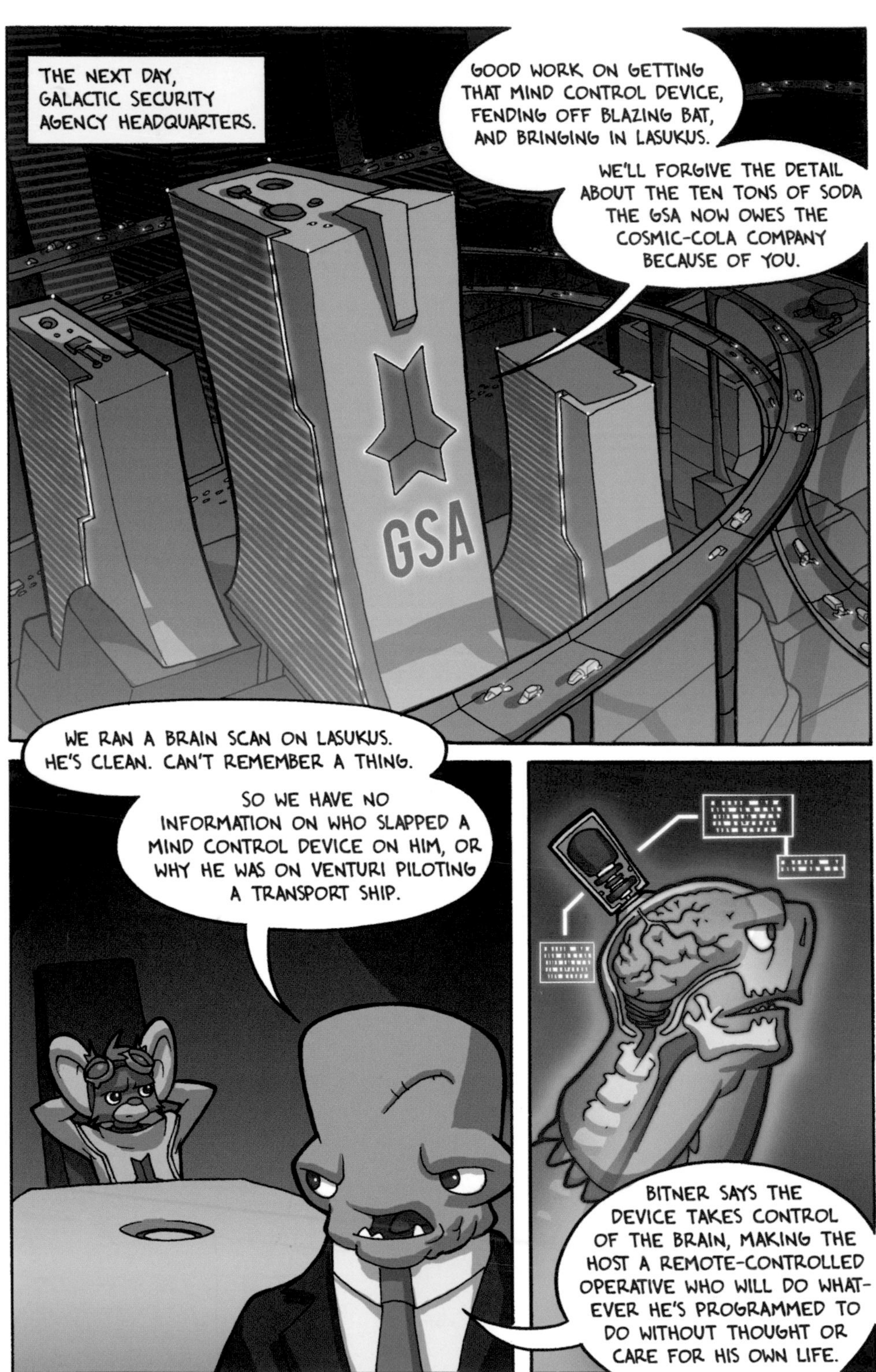
THE NEXT DAY, GALACTIC SECURITY AGENCY HEADQUARTERS.
GOOD WORK ON GETTING THAT MIND CONTROL DEVICE, FENDING OFF BLAZING BAT, AND BRINGING IN LASUKUS.
WE'LL FORGIVE THE DETAIL ABOUT THE TEN TONS OF SODA THE GSA NOW OWES THE COSMIC-COLA COMPANY BECAUSE OF YOU.
GSA
WE RAN A BRAIN SCAN ON LASUKUS. HE'S CLEAN. CAN'T REMEMBER A THING.
SO WE HAVE NO INFORMATION ON WHO SLAPPED A MIND CONTROL DEVICE ON HIM, OR WHY HE WAS ON VENTURI PILOTING A TRANSPORT SHIP.
BITNER SAYS THE DEVICE TAKES CONTROL OF THE BRAIN, MAKING THE HOST A REMOTE-CONTROLLED OPERATIVE WHO WILL DO WHAT-EVER HE'S PROGRAMMED TO DO WITHOUT THOUGHT OR CARE FOR HIS OWN LIFE.

WHICH WOULD MAKE HIM THE PERFECT TOOL FOR TRANSPORTING SOMETHING YOU DIDN'T WANT ANYONE TO KNOW ABOUT.
WE WEREN'T ABLE TO RETRIEVE THE SHIPMENT OF WHATEVER LASUKUS WAS TRANS-PORTING. IT WAS BLOWN UP, DESTROYING ALL THE EVIDENCE OF WHERE IT WAS FROM. THE BLAST SUGGESTS IT WAS DONE BY BLAZING BAT HIMSELF.

THERE'S SOMEBODY WHO DOESN'T WANT THE GSA TO FIND OUT WHAT'S GOING ON.

EXACTLY.
THE ONLY LEAD WE HAVE IS FROM LASUKUS. HE SAYS HE'S FROM THE OUTER COLONY WORLD OF TANKIUM3.
WE WANT YOU TO GO THERE.
RETURN LASUKUS, AND SEE IF YOU CAN GET TO THE BOTTOM OF WHO'S BEHIND THIS WHOLE ORDEAL AND WHAT THEY ARE SHIPPING TO VENTURI.
TANKIUM 3
TANKIUM 3

THAT'S A BIG JOB. I'LL NEED A GOOD TEAM OF AT LEAST FIVE AGENTS.

YOU'LL BE HEADING UP A TEAM OF SECURITY BOTS.

SECURITY BOTS?!! NO WAY, MAXWELL, I'M NOT WORKING WITH THOSE GUYS.

YOU KNOW THOSE GUYS ARE INEFFECTIVE. YOU'VE SEEN THE REPORTS.

THESE SECURITY BOTS ARE A TOOL. A PRODUCT OF YEARS OF DEVELOPMENT.

THEIR EFFECTIVENESS RESTS COMPLETELY IN THE HANDS OF WHOEVER IS USING THEM.

I'M NOT GOING TO LISTEN TO ANOTHER COMPLAINT. NOW GET OUT THERE AND SHOW ME HOW EFFECTIVE THESE BOTS CAN REALLY BE.
R-12

FINE.
SLAM!

TANKIUM3,
HOME PLANET OF LASUKUS.

GLAD TO BE HOME?
VERY MUCH SO!

TIME TO BOOT UP THE TIN CANS.

I WANT YOU ALL ON HIGH ALERT. FAN OUT AND FORM A PERIMETER AROUND THE CITY.

ROBOT 44, YOU COME WITH ME AS MY PERSONAL BACKUP.

THAT MEANS NO MATTER WHAT, YOU'VE GOT MY BACK.

GOT IT?

AFFIRMATIVE.

AH, FRESH AIR!

HELLO?!!! IT'S ME, LASUKUS!

THIS PLACE IS A GHOST TOWN.
IT'S SAFE! THEY ARE HERE TO HELP US!!

LASUKUS!!

OMNUS!!

LASUKUS, YOU'RE ALIVE!

BROTHER OMNUS! I AM GLAD YOU ARE ALIVE AS WELL!
WHO ARE THESE OFF-WORLDERS YOU BRING?

THIS IS MISSILE MOUSE. HE SAVED MY LIFE!

ON BEHALF OF MY PEOPLE, WE THANK YOU FOR SAVING OUR FRIEND AND BROTHER.
JUST DOING MY JOB.

WHERE IS EVERYBODY?

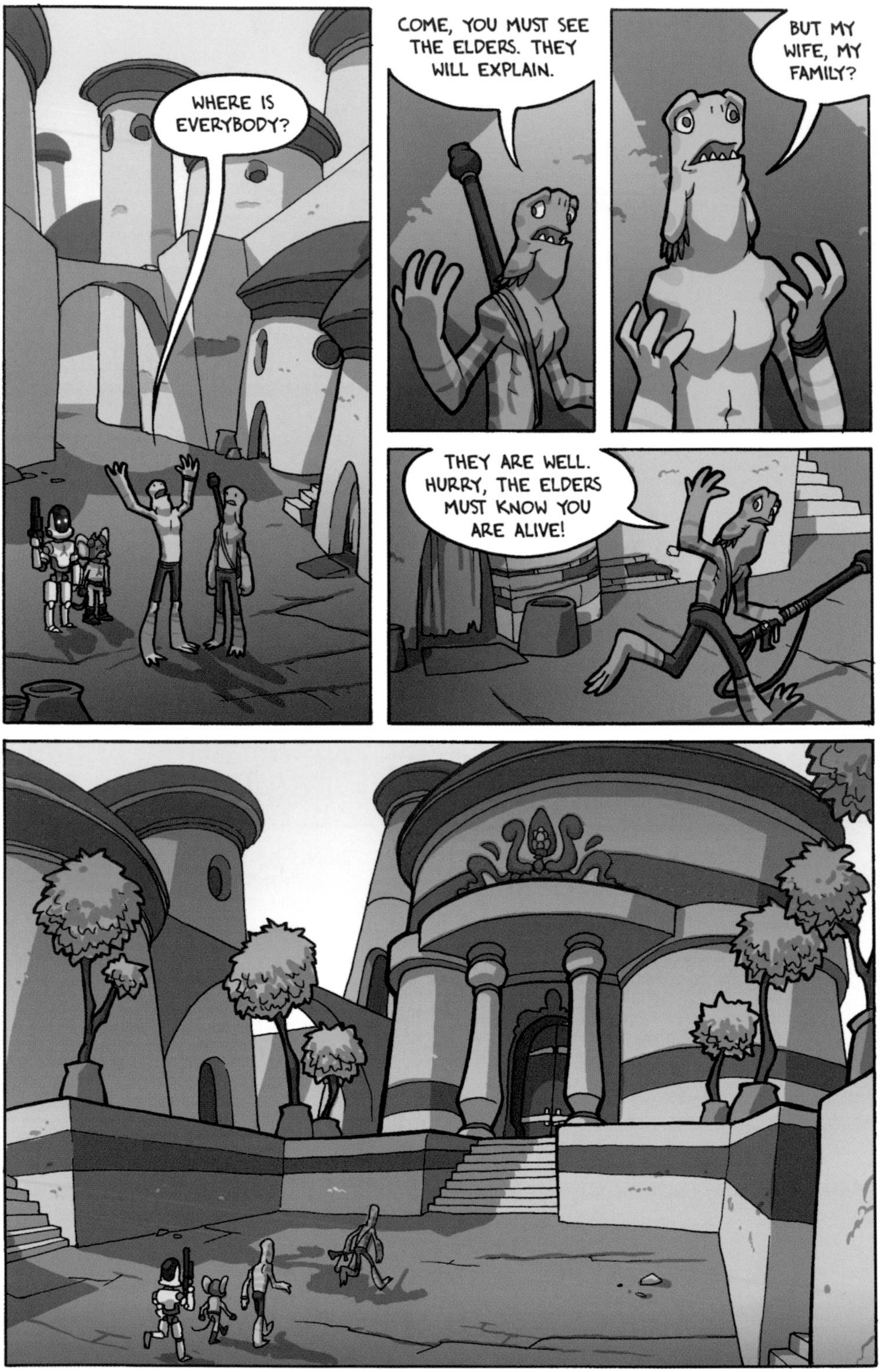

COME, YOU MUST SEE THE ELDERS. THEY WILL EXPLAIN.

BUT MY WIFE, MY FAMILY?

THEY ARE WELL. HURRY, THE ELDERS MUST KNOW YOU ARE ALIVE!

WHO ENTERS?
IT IS OMNUS. I BRING LASUKUS AND TWO OFF-WORLDERS, HERE TO HELP US.

LASUKUS! THANK THE GODS YOU HAVE RETURNED.

OFF-WORLDERS, TELL US WHO YOU ARE.

I AM MISSILE MOUSE OF THE GALACTIC SECURITY AGENCY.
AND THIS IS MY...MY...

I AM HIS BACKUP, HERE TO ASSIST HIM IN HELPING YOU.

WELCOME TO OUR CITY. WE THANK YOU FOR OFFERING YOUR HELP.

WE NEED TO KNOW WHAT HAPPENED HERE. WHY IS THE CITY DESOLATE? DO YOU KNOW WHO TOOK LASUKUS?

THE NIGHT LASUKUS WAS TAKEN, OUR CITY WAS RAIDED BY STRANGE OFF-WORLDERS.

THEY WENT HOUSE-TO-HOUSE AND TOOK EVERY ABLE-BODIED MAN.

THEY HAD STRANGE
POWERS THAT CAST A
SPELL ON OUR MEN...

THEY TOOK AWAY
THEIR WILL TO
FIGHT OR ESCAPE.

WE HAVE NOT SEEN
ANY OF THEM SINCE.

OUR WOMEN AND CHILDREN
HAVE BEEN SURVIVING ON
OUR STORAGES OF FOOD.

BUT THIS SUPPLY WILL
LAST ONLY UNTIL WINTER.

THE FEW MEN WHO WERE SPARED HAVE GONE SEARCHING FOR THE LOST MEN BUT HAVE FOUND NOTHING.

MISSILE MOUSE, YOU ARE OUR LAST HOPE.

ELDERS, I GIVE MY PROMISE THAT I WILL FIND AND RETURN YOUR MEN.

AS DO I!

THEN IT IS WITH GREAT HONOR THAT THE COUNCIL PETITIONS THE GODS OF PROTECTION ON YOUR BEHALF.

LASUKUS!

ALISSUS!!

YOU'RE ALIVE! OH, I WAS SO WORRIED.

THIS IS MISSILE MOUSE. HE SAVED ME AND BROUGHT ME HOME.

THEN TONIGHT WE FEAST IN YOUR HONOR!

THAT EVENING, IN THE HOME OF LASUKUS.

THAT WAS DELICIOUS, THANK YOU! I MIGHT ADD, YOU HAVE A FANTASTIC FAMILY.
THANK YOU.

THEY SEEM TO HAVE TAKEN A LIKING TO YOUR FRIEND.

HA HA HA HA HA
HA HA

MISSILE MOUSE, COME QUICK! YOUR ROBOTS ARE UNDER ATTACK AND THE TRANSPORT IS DESTROYED!

44, LET'S GO!

HIDE THE CHILDREN IN THE CELLAR. I'LL BE BACK!

THIS IS THE WORK OF...

THE BLAZING BAT?
PRECISELY.

YOU'RE MINE, MOUSE!

THEN COME DOWN HERE AND GET ME!
I DON'T HAVE TO.
BEEP!

SHHHICK
SHHHIIICK

GAH!

MISSILE MOUSE!

FFSHOOM

FWOOSH!!

CHOOM!

POOMF!

TINK

INITIATE TRACKING.

SHOOOOM

I NEED ONE OF YOUR ANIMALS.

IF YOU'RE GOING AFTER HIM, I'M COMING WITH YOU.

YOU DO SO AT YOUR OWN RISK.

THEN I BETTER START PREPPING THEM FOR OUR JOURNEY.

LATER...
I'VE LOST YOU ONCE, I CAN'T BEAR TO LOSE YOU AGAIN!
I MUST GO. HE SAVED MY LIFE, I OWE IT TO HIM TO SAVE HIS.

AND HE IS THE ONLY HOPE WE HAVE OF RETURNING OUR BROTHERS HOME.

I PROMISE I'LL RETURN.
HEY!

HUG AND KISS...?!

HA-HA! I WOULDN'T FORGET YOU GUYS!
HUG!
KISS!
HUG!
HUG!
KISS!
KISS!
KISS!

ARE YOU READY?
AFFIRMATIVE.

MEANWHILE, AT THE FORTRESS OF KING BOGNARSH...

HA-HAAA! EXCELLENT WORK, BLAZING BAT.

HERE'S YOUR CASH.

YOU SHOULD STAY FOR MY FEAST THIS EVENING. YOU'VE EARNED IT.

THANK YOU.

SO, MISSILE MOUSE, I'VE HEARD A LOT ABOUT YOU.
FUNNY, NEVER HEARD OF *YOU* BEFORE.
HA! THAT'S HOW I LIKE IT.

NAME'S BOGNARSH... KING BOGNARSH. I RULE THIS PLANET.
CAME HERE A FEW YEARS AGO AND DECIDED I HAD TO HAVE IT.

BUT I KEEP A LOW PROFILE.

DON'T WANT THE GSA FIDDLING AROUND IN MY BUSINESS.

AND WHAT BUSINESS WOULD THAT BE?

WHY, **STARDUST**, OF COURSE!
STARDUST?

IT'S THE SECRET INGREDIENT OF COSMIC-COLA. SUPPOSEDLY MAKES IT THE MOST REFRESHING DRINK IN THE GALAXY. ALL I KNOW IS, THIS IS THE ONLY PLANET YOU CAN FIND IT ON.
AND SINCE I'M THEIR ONLY SUPPLIER, COSMIC-COLA CAN'T MEET THE DEMAND FOR THEIR DRINK WITHOUT ME!
A RARE SUBSTANCE, AND AN AMPLE SUPPLY OF SLAVE LABOR...
...IT'S THE PERFECT MONEYMAKING MACHINE!
MIND-CONTROLLED SLAVES! YOU'RE SICK, BOGNARSH!

YOU THINK THEY'D WORK FOR FREE ANY OTHER WAY?

ALL RIGHT, YOU'RE BORING ME.

HMMMM...

GUARDS!

TELL YOU WHAT, SINCE YOU'RE SO INTERESTED IN MY MINING OPERATION, HOW ABOUT YOU EXPERIENCE IT FIRSTHAND WHILE I DECIDE WHAT TO DO WITH YOU.

BOOM

AH!

GAAAAAA!

AS YOU WISH, ALMIGHTY BOGNARSH.

MEANWHILE, TWO DAYS INTO THEIR JOURNEY...
LET'S TOUCH DOWN OVER THERE!

WE'RE CLOSE.

WE'LL HAVE TO HIKE IN FROM HERE.

MY READINGS SAY WE HAVE TO CROSS A CANYON.
NO, NOT A CANYON...
A SLAVE PIT!

INTERESTING.
WHAT IS IT?

THAT ANTENNA ARRAY IS TRANSMITTING SIGNALS TO EACH OF THE SLAVES, TELLING THEM WHAT TO DO.

DESTROY IT AND YOUR BROTHERS WILL BE SET FREE.

THIS SHOULD BE ENOUGH.

BUT WHAT ABOUT MISSILE MOUSE?
YOU JUST WORRY ABOUT DESTROYING THAT TRANSMITTER. LEAVE HIM TO ME.

DID YOU HEAR? KING BOGNARSH IS CUTTING OUR PAY AGAIN.

SAYS IT'S BECAUSE OF TOUGH ECONOMIC TIMES OR SOMETHING...

THAT'S A LOAD OF NAGBUT SPIT! HE'S HAD HIS MOST PROFITABLE YEAR YET...

EXCUSE ME...

HEY! WHO ARE YOU?!!

THUNK!
THUNK!

WE ARE YOUR SLAVES.
WHAT DO YOU REQUIRE?

STAY ON THE FLOOR.
YOUR WISH...
...IS OUR COMMAND.

central database

#332456 aka Missile Mouse
status: SLAVE
location: sector 12
HE'S BEEN MADE A SLAVE?!

IF I LOCK ONTO THE FREQUENCY OF HIS MIND CONTROL DEVICE, IT WILL LEAD ME STRAIGHT TO HIM!

POW

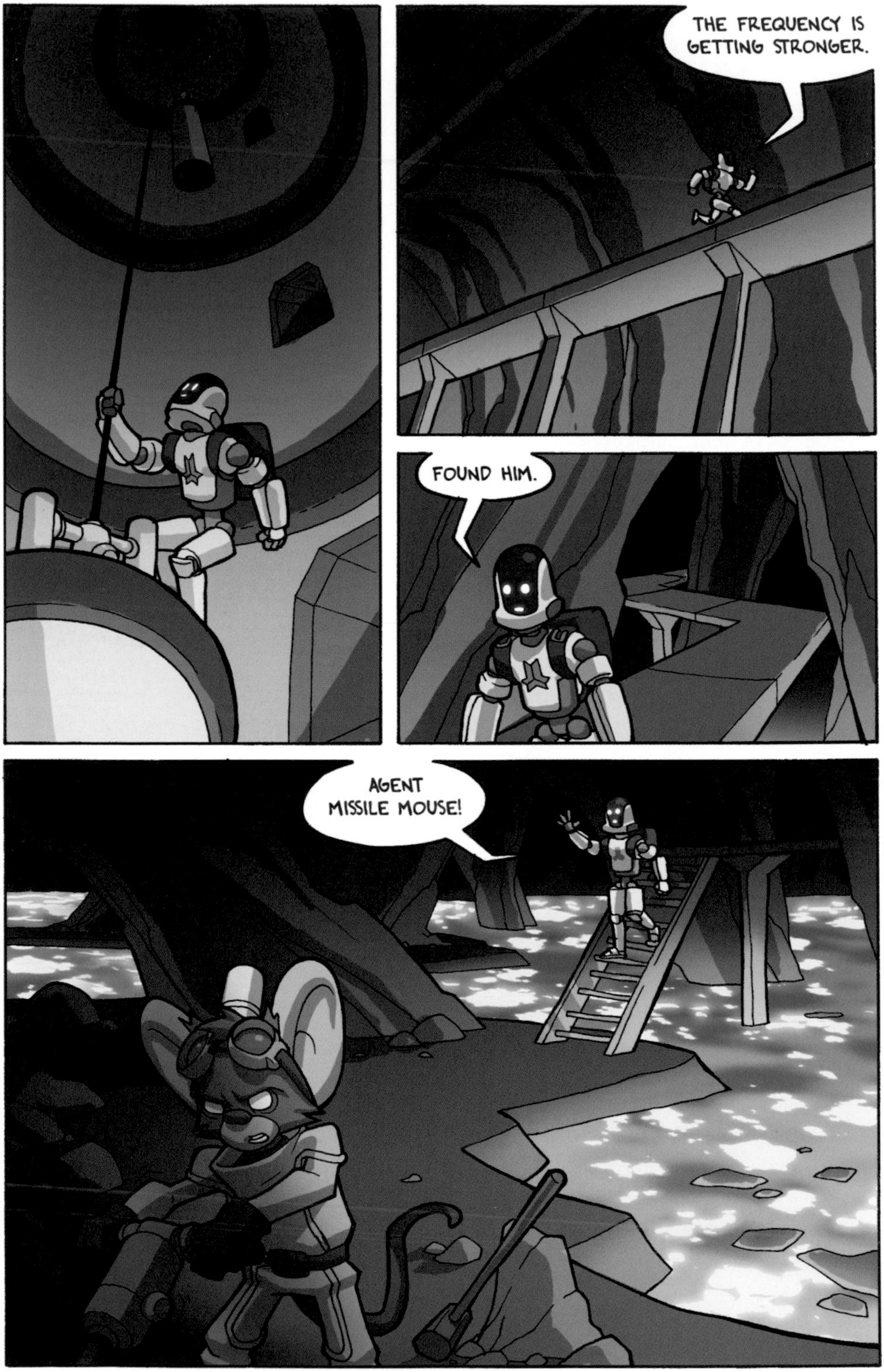

AGENT MISSILE MOUSE!

INTRUDER! YOU WILL BE ELIMINATED!

MISSILE MOUSE! IT IS I, ROBOT 44!

CLANG!

WHACK!

BAM!
WHIP!

CHACK!

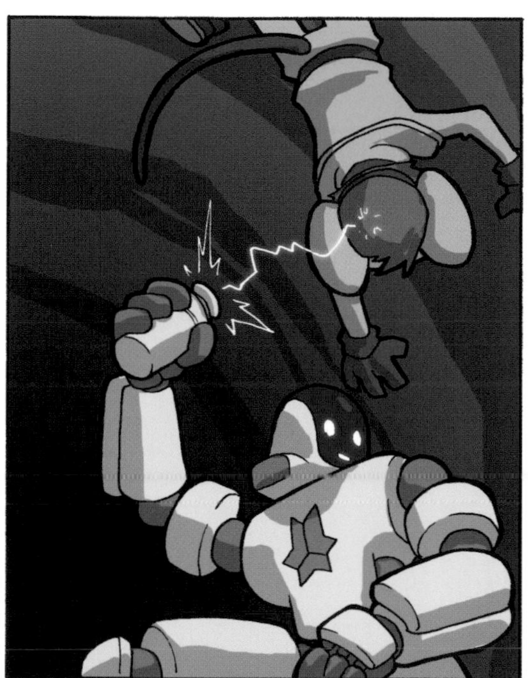

WUMP!

44...WHAT'S GOING ON?

YOU HAD A MIND CONTROL DEVICE ATTACHED TO YOU.

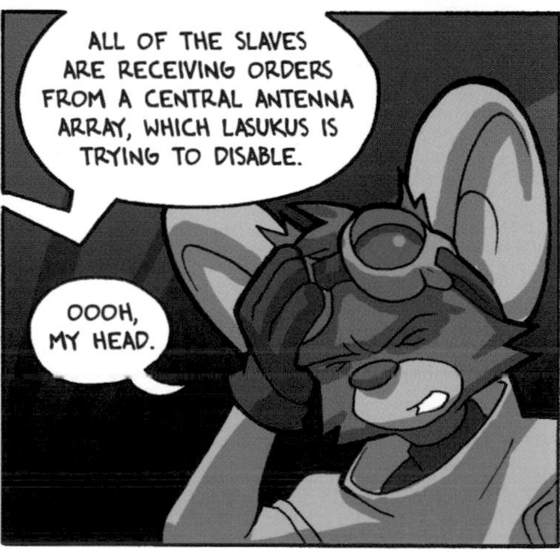
ALL OF THE SLAVES ARE RECEIVING ORDERS FROM A CENTRAL ANTENNA ARRAY, WHICH LASUKUS IS TRYING TO DISABLE.
OOOH, MY HEAD.

HERE, I THOUGHT YOU WOULD WANT THESE.

THANKS, 44!

RUMMMMBBBLLEEERUMMMMBBE

RAAARRR

KRASH!

BLAM

BLAM
BLAM
BLAM
LOOKS LIKE BLASTERS ARE INEFFECTIVE!

MISSILE MOUSE, YOUR MIND CONTROLLER!
ATTACH IT TO ITS HEAD, UNDER THE ARMOR!

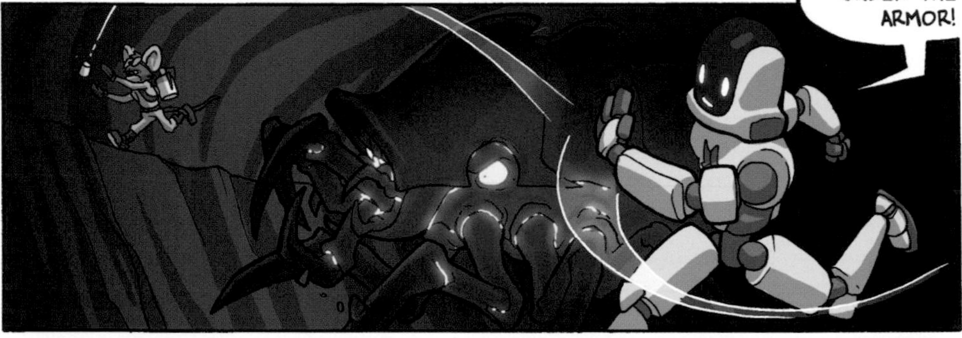

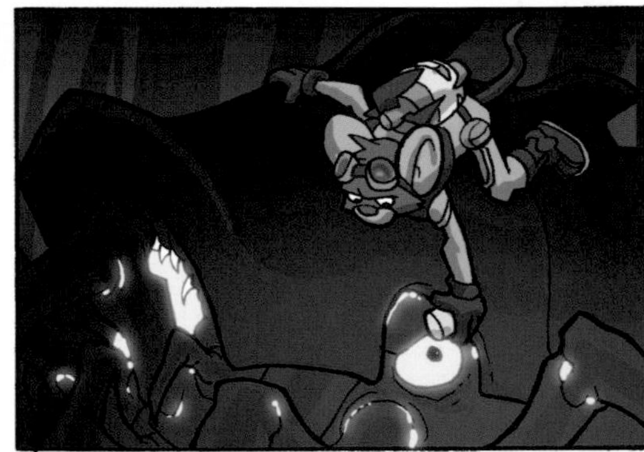

WHOA!

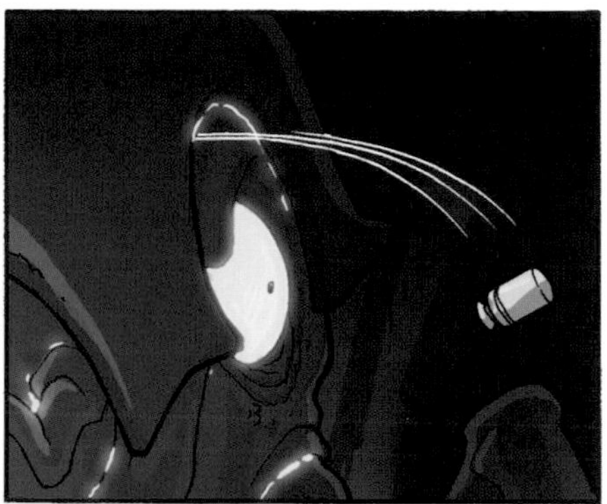

GAH!
IT DIDN'T
STICK!

SMASH!

ANY
OTHER
IDEAS?

SO HE SAYS TO ME, "PLEASE, YOU'VE TAKEN ALL THAT I HAVE!" HA-HA, LIKE HE THOUGHT I WOULD CARE.
EXCUSE M-ME, MISSILE MOUSE JUST WENT OFF-LINE. HE'S FREE!

HE WHAT?!!

SMASH!

KONK

BLAZING BAT! FINISH THIS MOUSE GUY OFF.
MY PLEASURE.

CLINK!

CLICK CLICK

BEEP!

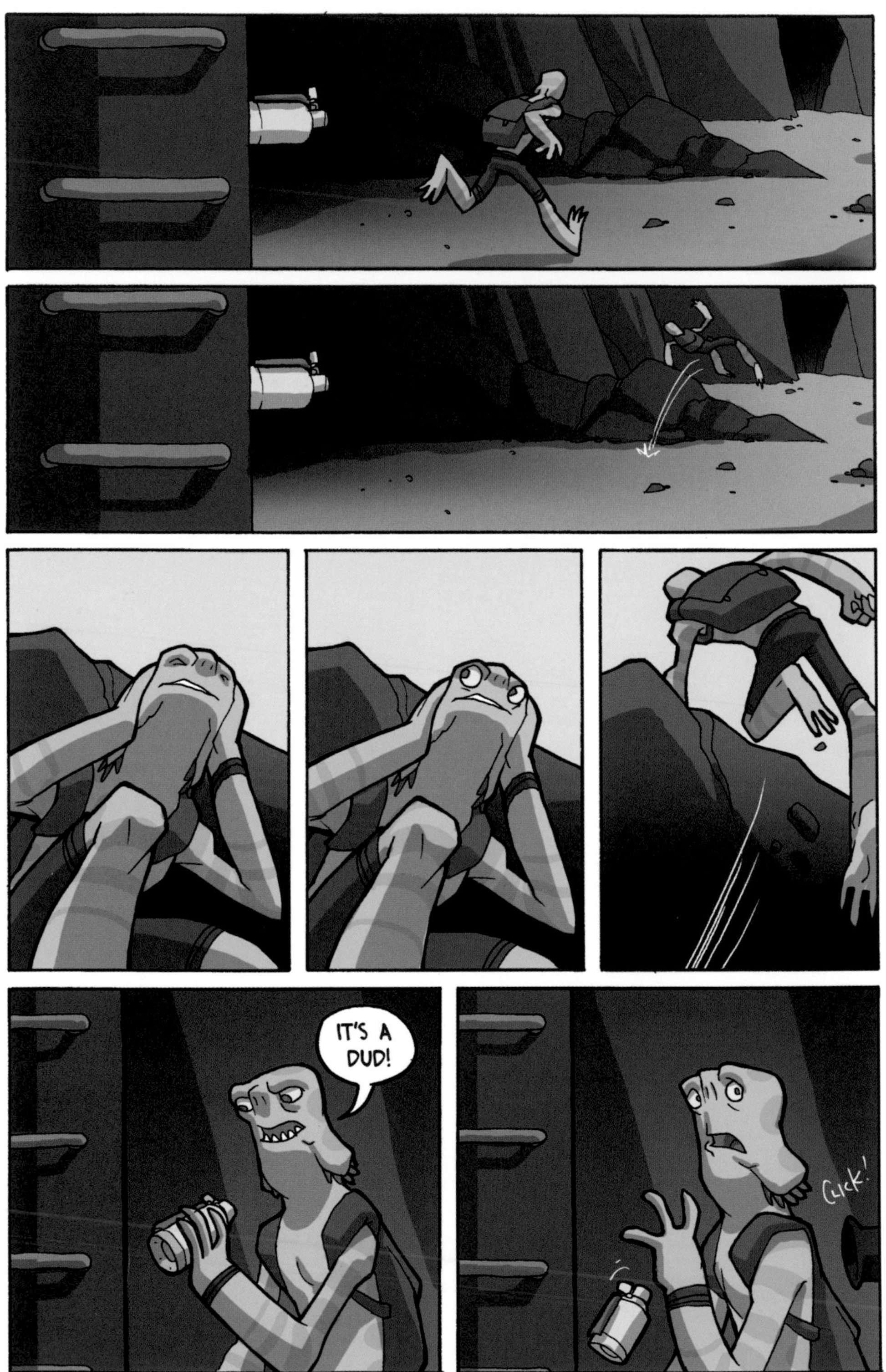
IT'S A DUD!
CLICK!

JUST WHAT DO YOU THINK YOU'RE DOING?

I...UH...I'M CHECKING THE ANTENNA FOR PROPER...UH... CONNECTIVITY.

YEAH, RIGHT. YOU'RE COMING WITH US!

C'MON, MOVE IT!
NUDGE

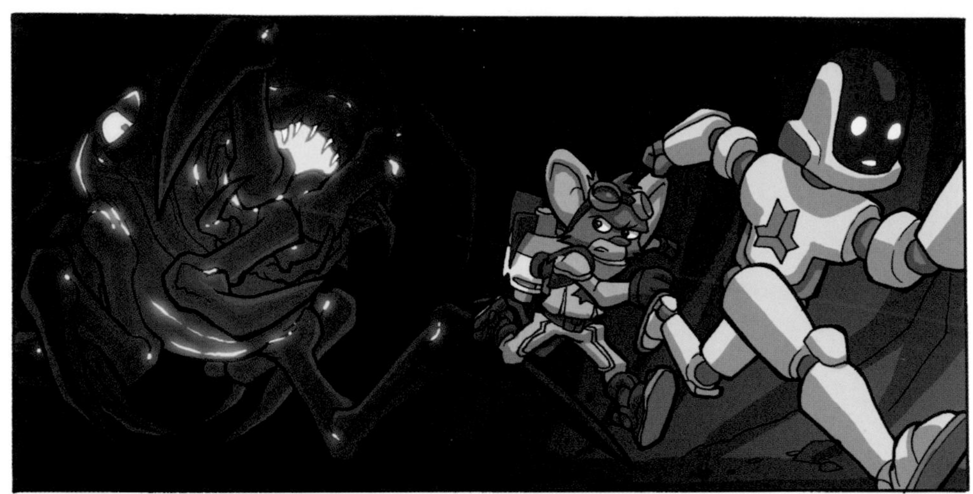

LOOK!

THAT PIPE CARRIES A COOLANT FOR THE UNDER-GROUND COOLING SYSTEM.

ARE YOU THINKING WHAT I'M THINKING?

AFFIRMATIVE. I'LL CREATE THE DIVERSION.

HALT, BEAST!

NOT A LOT OF TIME TO BUILD UP PRESSURE!

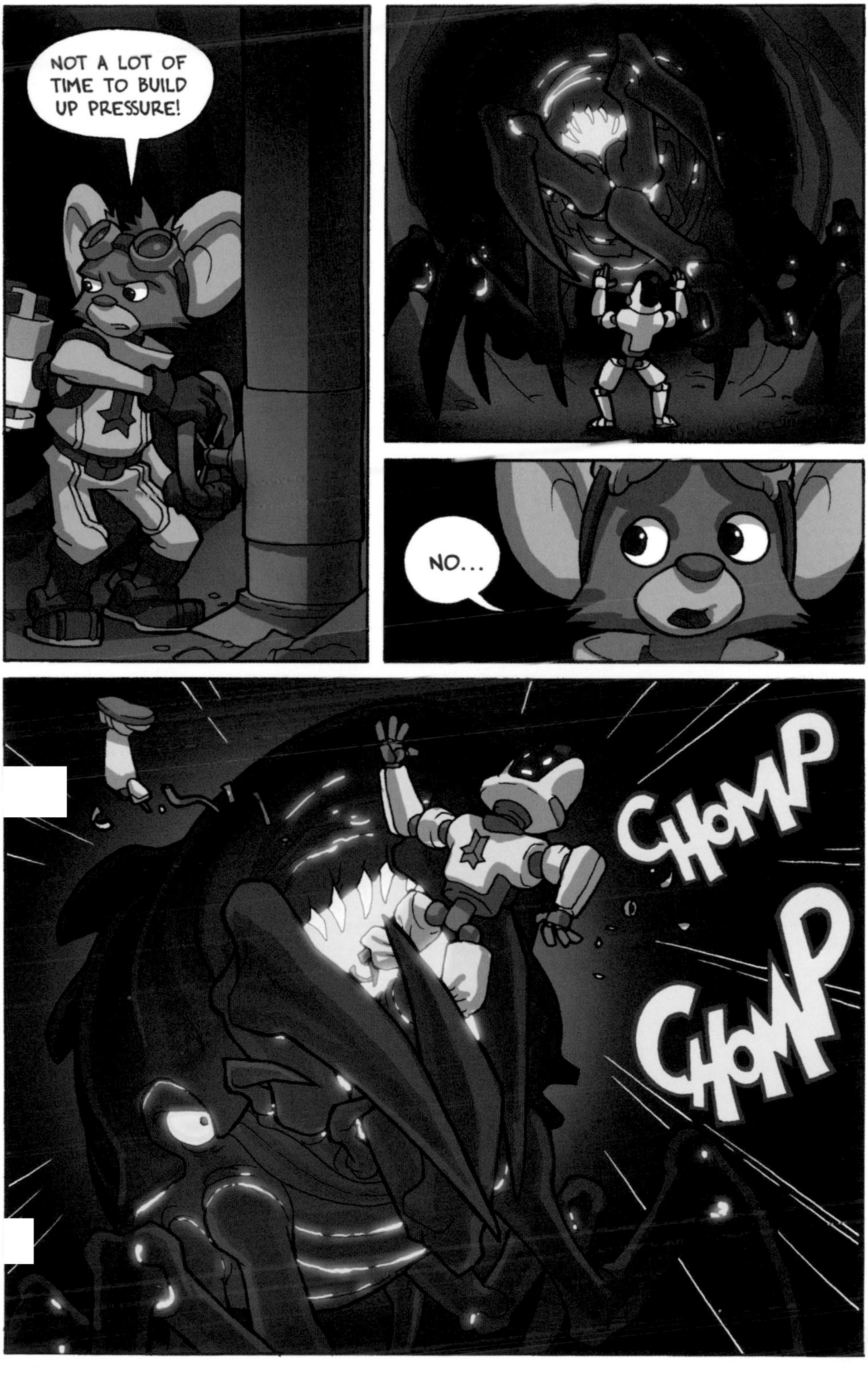

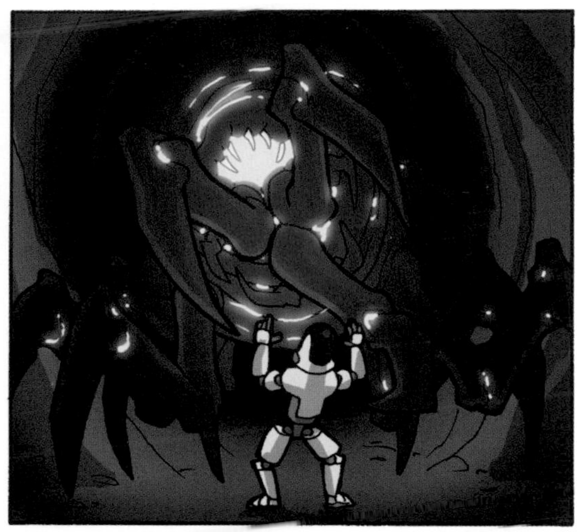

NO...

CHOMP
CHOMP

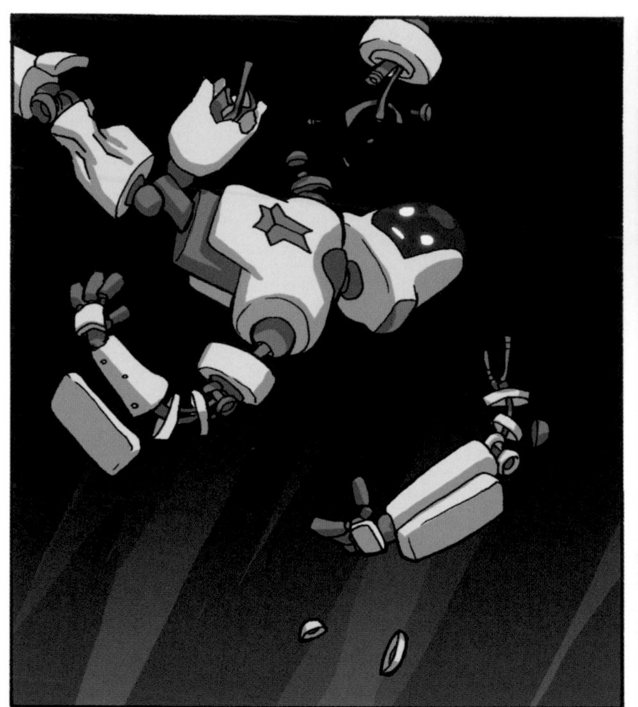

CLUNK!

NOOOOOOOOO

COME AND GET ME, YA OVERGROWN COCKROACH!
SSSSSsss
SSSs
SSSs

BRANG!

BOOM

44!

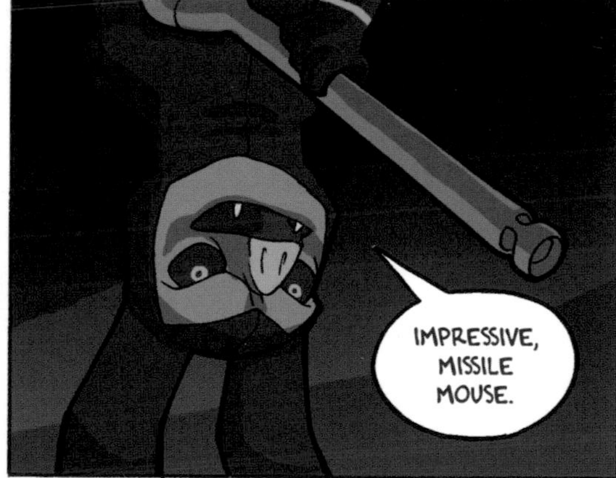
IMPRESSIVE, MISSILE MOUSE.

BWOOSH

SHOOT, WHERE'S MY BLASTER?!

DANG IT!

FWOOSH
HEY! THAT WAS MY FAVORITE BLASTER!
FAWOOSH

WOW, THIS SHELL ABSORBED THE HEAT!

COME OUT AND PLAY, MISSILE MOUSE!

YOU KEEP RUINING MY TOYS!

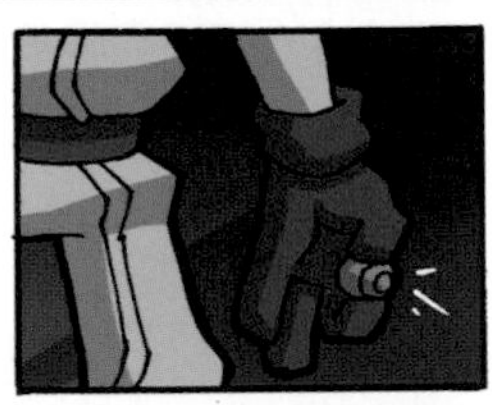

Whip!

SPASH!!

FRAAASH

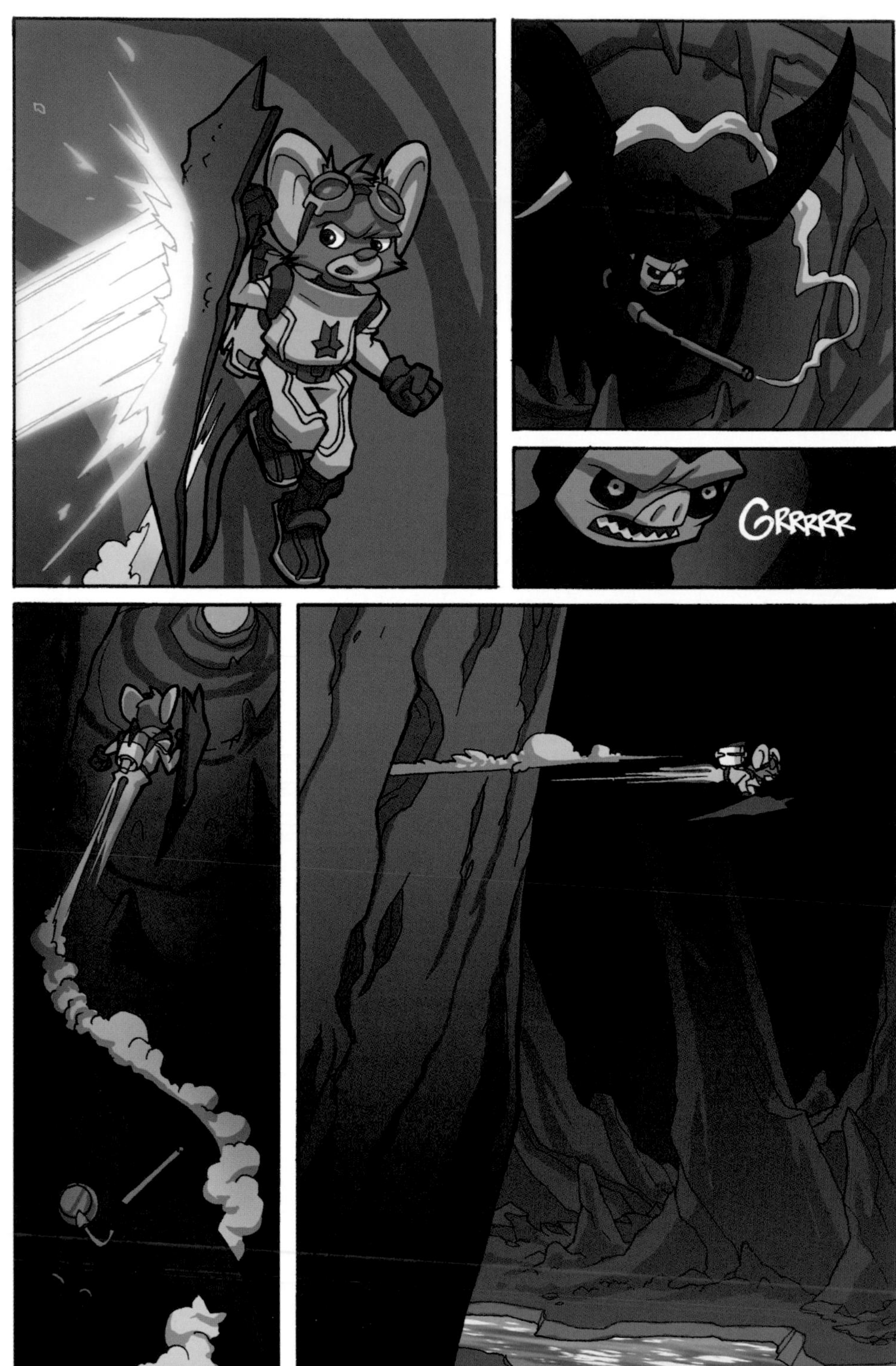
GRRRRR

AH!

GOT TO FIND AN ESCAPE ROUTE!

GAH, DEAD END!

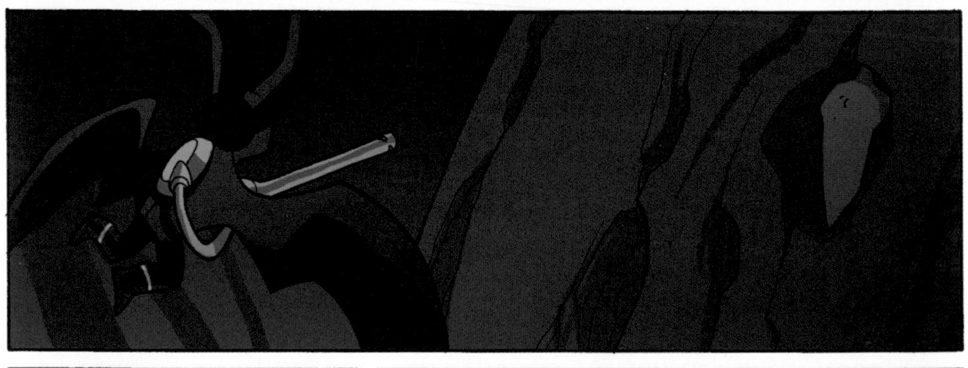

CHIC-KAH

MAN, THAT'S GETTING HOT!

TOO...HOT...

FFRUSHHHH

KEEP IT MOVIN'.

ALL RIGHT, THIS IS YOUR HOME UNTIL WE CAN GET YOU ANOTHER MIND CONTROL DEVICE.

SMACK!

GRRRR

OF COURSE, THAT'S IF ANYONE REMEMBERS YOU'RE DOWN HERE.

Huf
Huf

WAM!

YOU'LL REGRET THAT ONE!
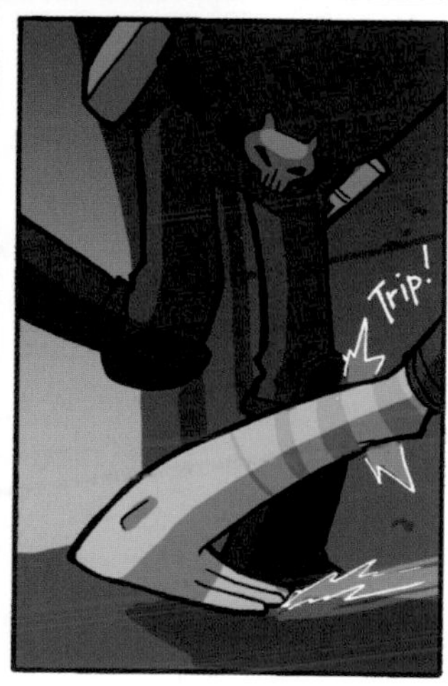
Trip!

FRAZZZ

ZZZZ
CLANK

YOU CAN'T DO THIS!

PERFECT.

WHEN I GET MY HANDS ON YOU, I'LL...

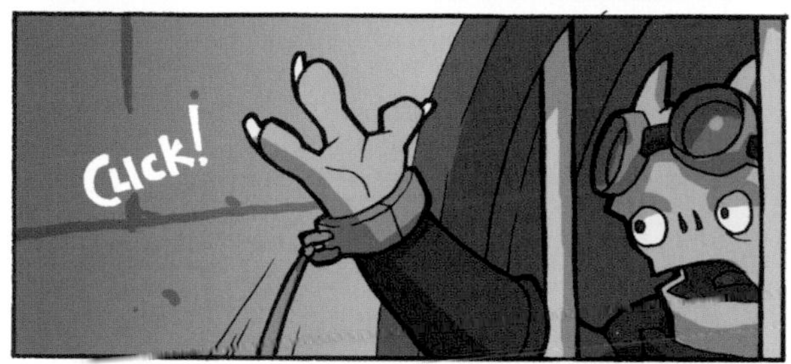
CLICK!

CLICK

WHEN BOGNARSH FINDS OUT WHAT YOU DID TO US, YOU'LL WISH YOU WERE NEVER BORN!

OF COURSE, THAT'S IF HE EVER FINDS OUT YOU TWO ARE DOWN HERE.

HEY! GET BACK HERE!
WHAT HAPPENED?

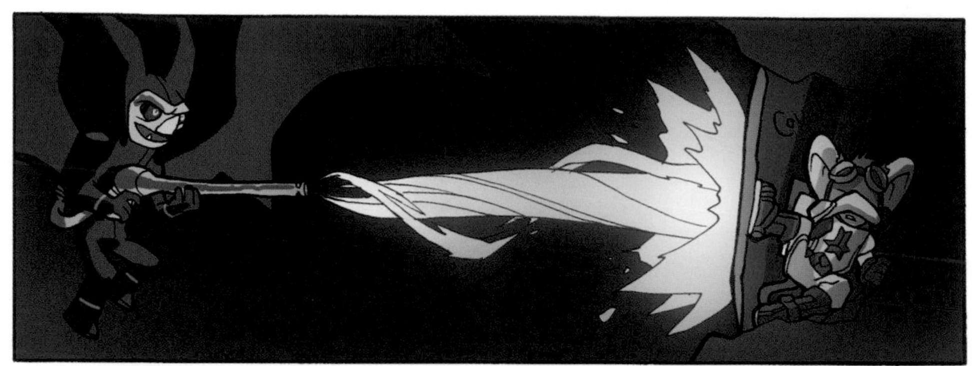

OOH - CAN'T -COUGH- HOLD ON...

HAHAHA HA

SMACK!

?

44!
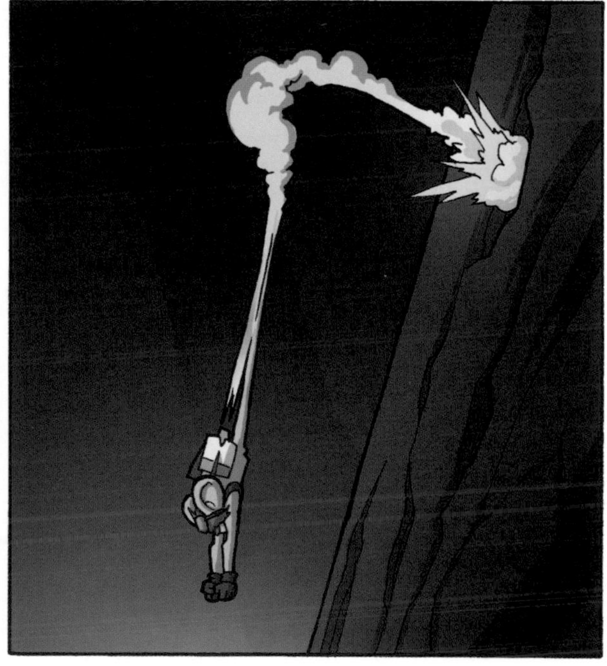

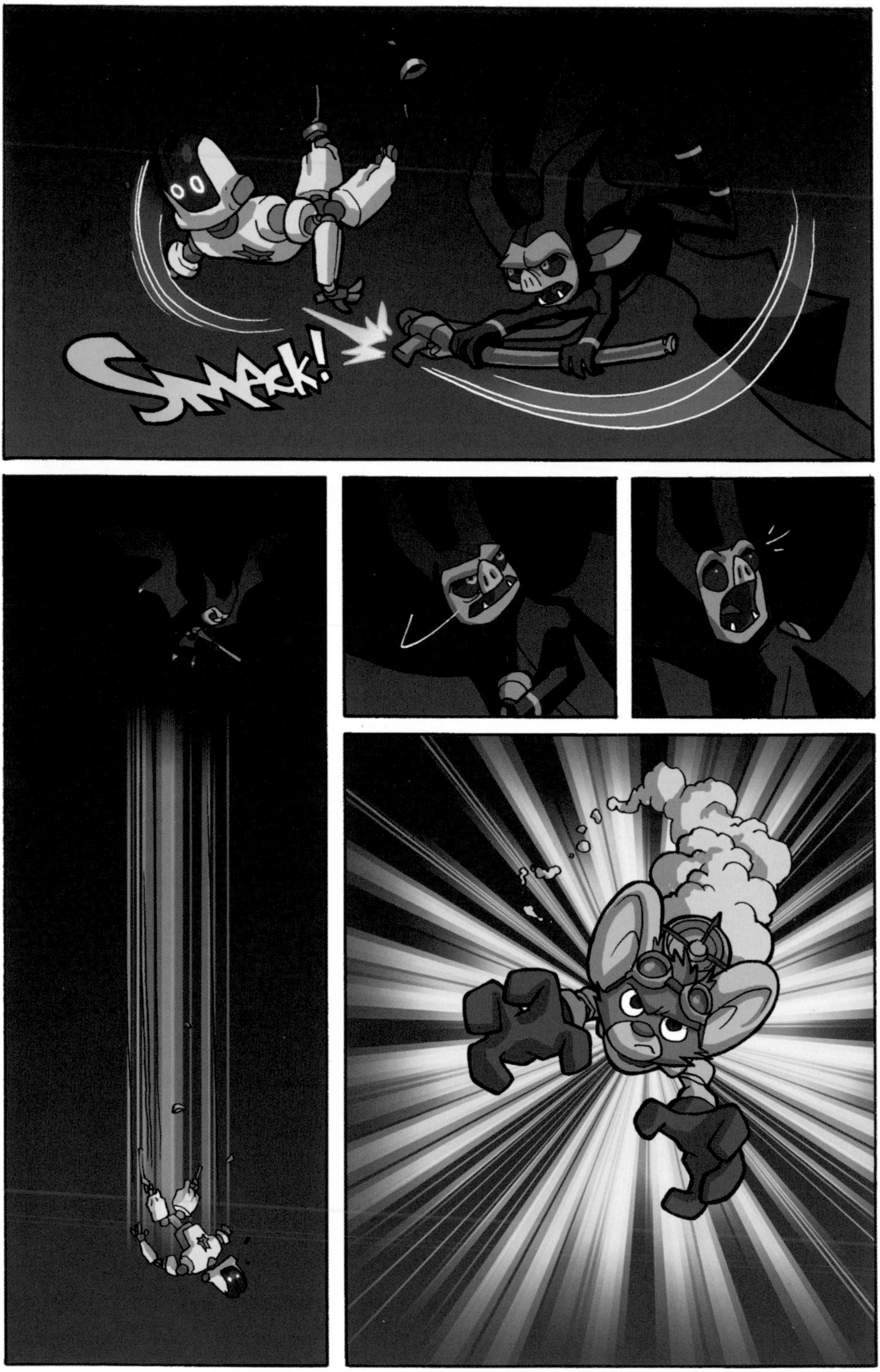

SMACK!

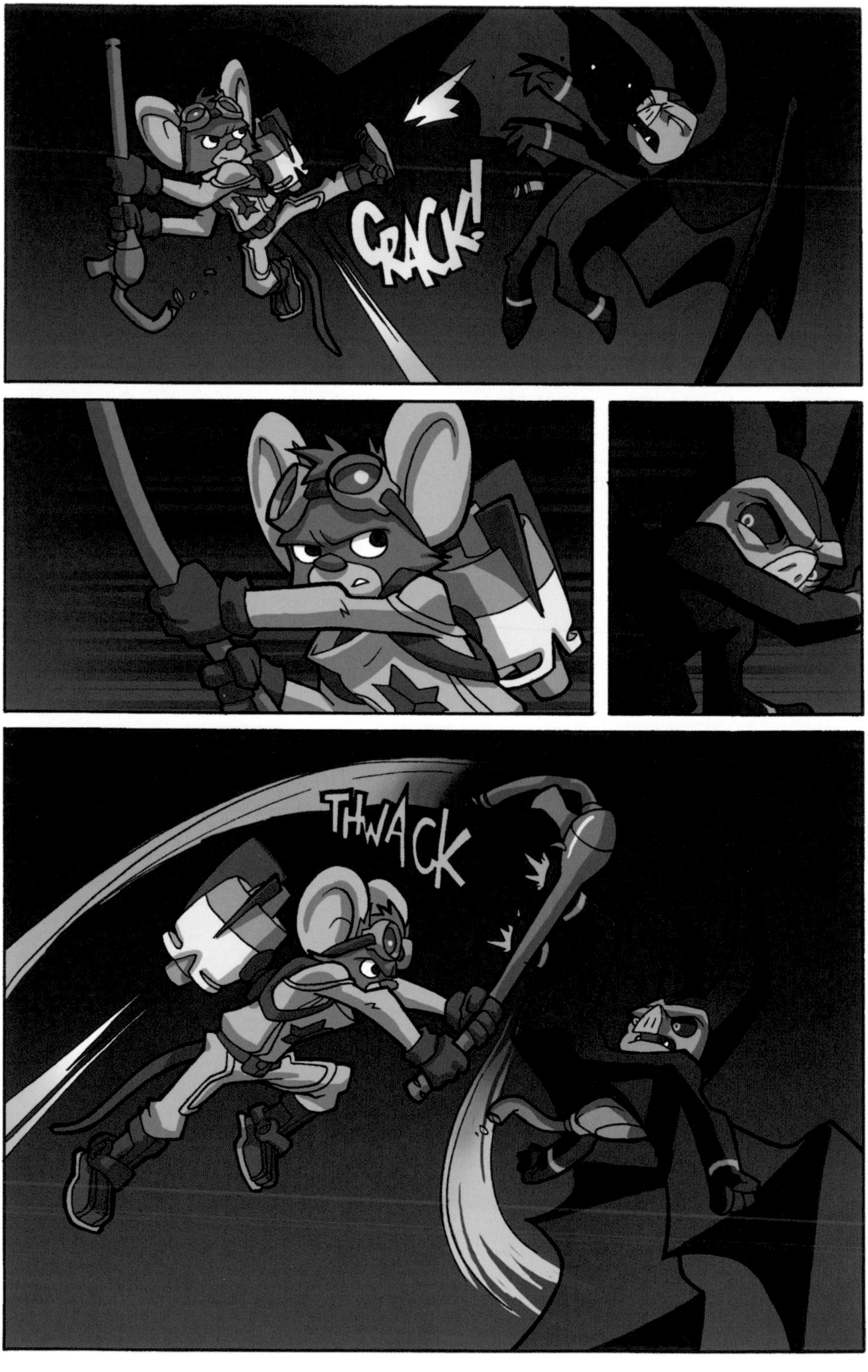

THWACK

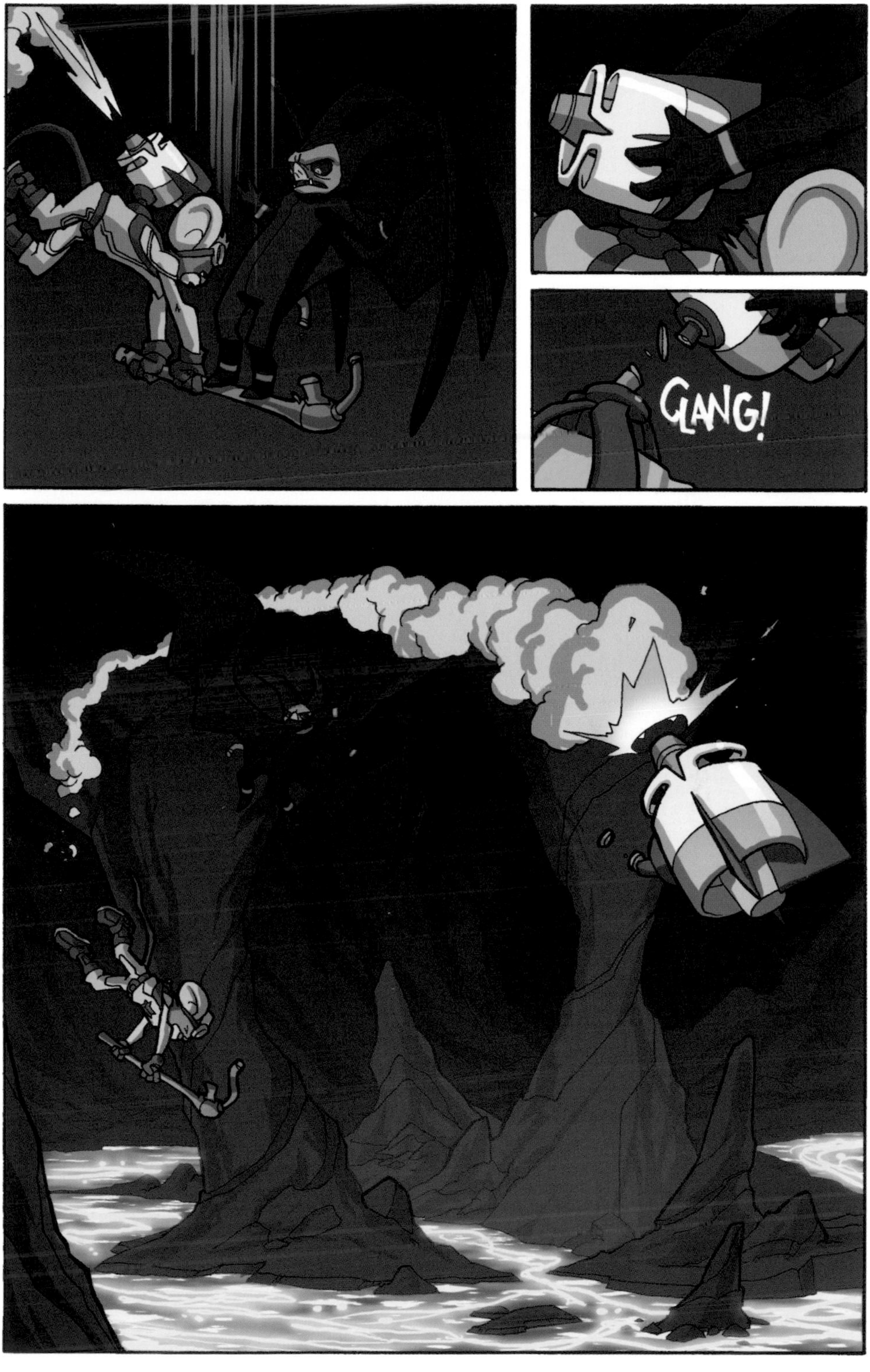

CLANG!

MISSION FINALLY ACCOMPLISHED! HA-HA-HA!

HUFF
HUFF

GRRRRR

MISSION FAILED, BLAZING BAT!

WHAT DO YOU THINK YOU'RE DOING?!

BRINGING YOU DOWN, BLAZING BAT!

YOU MAKE MY JOB TOO EASY!

WAY TOO EASY.

BLOP

CLICK

WHA-?
WHIP
WHIP

WHIIIP!

KONK

GAHHH

GAH! YOU'LL PAY FOR THAT!

THIS IS IT, MOUSE. YOU'RE NOT GOING ANYWHERE!

WE FINISH THIS HERE AND NOW!

RUMMMBBLLERUMBBLLRUMMMB

!
BLLRUMMMB

YOU'RE THE ONE WHO'S FINISHED!

HEY! WHERE DO YOU THINK YOU'RE GOING?!
NICE KNOWING YOU, BLAZING BAT.
GET BACK HERE AND FIGHT, YA RAT!

RUMMMBBLLERUMBBLLLRUMMMBRUMM
?
LERUMBBLLLRUMMMBRUMM

HUH?

AAHH!

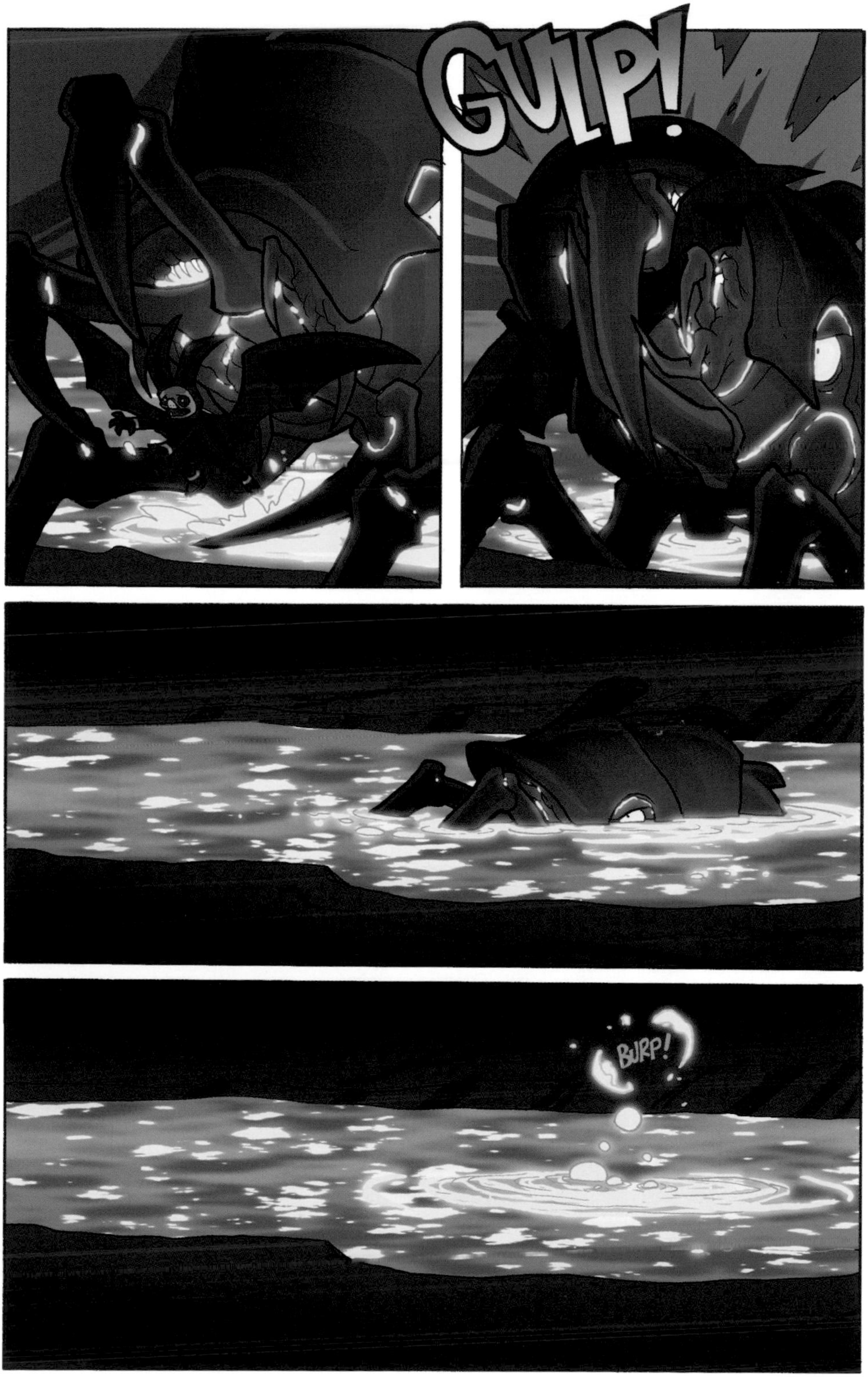

GULP!

ZZ
ZZZ ZZ ZZZZ ZZZZ

KING BOGNARSH.

SNORT

AHEM, BOGNARSH!

IT'S MY TURN TO RIDE THE PONY!
I AM *SO* SORRY TO INTERRUPT.
HUH...WHAT? WHAT IS IT?

WE'VE LOST OUR SIGNAL FROM BLAZING BAT. MISSILE MOUSE ELIMINATED HIM, SIR.

WHAT??! GOOD-FOR-NOTHING BOUNTY HUNTER!

SNAG

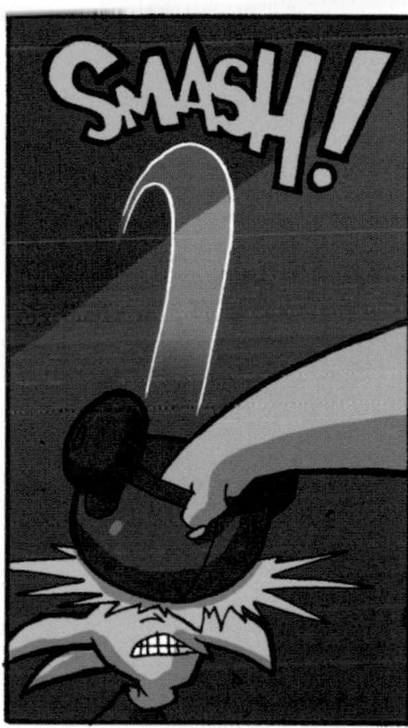
SMASH!

OK...OK...SWITCH THE SLAVES TO HUNT-AND-KILL MODE. SEND THEM AFTER MISSILE MOUSE AND HIS GANG.

AND MAKE SURE THAT MONEY WE PAID BLAZING BAT GOES BACK IN THE VAULT.
YES, SIR.

44!

44, YOU'RE A MESS! LET'S GET YOU OUT OF HERE.

NO...MISSILE MOUSE, YOU HAVE TO FINISH THE MISSION.

NOT WITHOUT YOU!

COME ON.

WE'LL GET YOU BACK TO BITNER AND HAVE YOU FIXED UP IN NO TIME.

AH, BRIGHT!

BACK, OFF, GUYS!

HOLD ON,
44!

I HOPE LASUKUS
IS DOING BETTER
THAN WE ARE!

STOP!
I AM YOUR
BROTHER!!

CRACK!

LET'S HOPE THIS WORKS!
CLICK

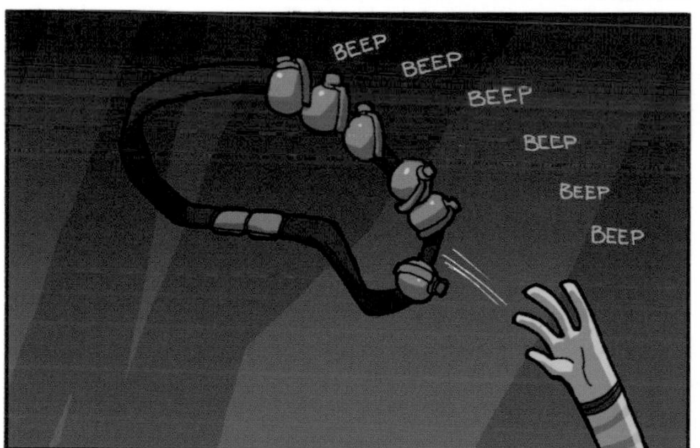
BEEP
BEEP
BEEP
BEEP
BEEP
BEEP

BEEP
BEEP
BEEP
BEEP
BEEP

BOOM!

POP

WHERE AM I?

WHAT ARE WE DOING HERE?
WHAT HAS HAPPENED TO US?
WHERE ARE WE?
WHAT'S GOING ON?
WHERE IS MY FAMILY?
WHAT IS THIS?

MISSILE MOUSE!
YOU'RE ALIVE!

LASUKUS, YOU DID IT! YOU FREED YOUR PEOPLE!

NO...NOT YET.

WHERE'RE YOU GOING?
WE STILL HAVE A LITTLE HOUSE-CLEANING TO DO!

BROTHERS, LISTEN TO ME! THE NIGHT OUR HOMES WERE INVADED AND WE WERE TORN FROM OUR FAMILIES, OUR MINDS WERE ALSO TAKEN FROM US.

WE WERE MADE SLAVES. MADE TO ENDURE BACK-BREAKING HARDSHIP IN HORRIBLE CAVES...

...WHILE THOSE WHO BROUGHT THIS UPON US LIVED IN LUXURY HIGH ABOVE US.

BUT THEY WERE FOOLISH TO THINK THEY COULD GET AWAY WITH THIS. WE WILL BRING JUSTICE TO THEIR DOORSTEP!

OUR NUMBERS ARE GREAT AND OUR WILL STRONG! LET'S MAKE THEM WISH THEY NEVER STEPPED FOOT ON OUR EARTH!
RAAAAAAA RAAAAA RAAAA
RAAAA

OH NO, THEY'RE STORMING THE PALACE!!

YOU THERE! TAKE US TO YOUR LEADER, OR ELSE!

MY LEADER?

I'D BE HAPPY TO! BUT FIRST WE NEED TO GET YOU SOME WEAPONS!

? ? ? ? ?
FOLLOW ME.

THERE YOU ARE! OK, 44, LET'S GET YOU HOME.

44?

HE'S... HE'S...DEAD.

HEY, BOGNARSH!

DO YOU *WANT* TO DIE? BECAUSE I THOUGHT YOU KNEW BETTER THAN TO INTERRUPT "ME" TIME.

I JUST WANTED TO LET YOU KNOW WE HAVE SOME VISITORS.

"ME" TIME IS *OVER*, BOGNARSH!
pop

MOTHER, WHEN IS FATHER COMING HOME?

I...I DON'T KNOW.

OH...

BUT YOUR FATHER MADE A PROMISE THAT HE'D RETURN...

AND HE'S NEVER BROKEN A PROMISE.

WE'D BETTER GET BREAKFAST READY BEFORE THE OTHER KIDS GET UP.

MOM!

IT'S THE EVIL MEN, COME TO TAKE THE REST OF US!

NO, LOOK!

LASUKUS!

DADDY'S BACK!
DADDY'S BACK!!

I TOLD YOU I'D RETURN.
HUG!
KISS!
HUG!

I MUST GO REPORT TO THE ELDERS NOW.

LATER...
LOOK AT OUR PEOPLE, LASUKUS!
SO HAPPY!

INDEED.
AND WE HAVE YOU TWO TO THANK FOR THIS.

AND, MISSILE MOUSE, I AM SORRY TO HEAR OF THE DEATH OF YOUR FRIEND.

HE SERVED HONORABLY.

THANK YOU.

IT LOOKS LIKE NOT EVERYBODY IS TOO HAPPY WITH THE OUTCOME!
YOU CAN'T DO THIS TO ME! I'M A **KING**! A ***KING***, I SAY!!

KONK

HEY!

THIS IS KIND OF FUN!

SMASH
HAHAHAHA

MISSILE MOUSE, TONIGHT WE CELEBRATE THE RETURN OF OUR MEN. WILL YOU JOIN US?

THANK YOU. BUT I MUST GET ROBOT 44 HOME TO SEE IF HE CAN BE REPAIRED.

I UNDERSTAND. MAY THE SUN ALWAYS SHINE ON YOUR PATH.

AND KNOW THAT YOU ALWAYS HAVE A HOME HERE.

THANK YOU, MISSILE MOUSE, FOR EVERYTHING.

TAKE CARE, LASUKUS.

ONE WEEK LATER.

THE GSA COUNCIL FOR OPERATIONS.

...IN CONCLUSION, THE TANKIUM PEOPLE HAVE PROVED THEMSELVES TO BE STRONG...

...AND WITH THE STARDUST MINES NOW UNDER THEIR CONTROL, THEY SHOW SIGNS OF FUTURE PROSPERITY.

DESPITE LOSING AN ENTIRE SQUAD OF GSA ROBOTS, GOOD WORK, AGENT MISSILE MOUSE. MISSION ACCOMPLISHED.
I HAVE ONE LAST THING TO SAY ABOUT ROBOT 44.

I'VE SERVED WITH A LOT OF AGENTS ON A LOT OF MISSIONS, AND ROBOT 44 WAS NO LESS HEROIC, LOYAL, OR CAPABLE THAN ANY OF THOSE AGENTS.
DETAILS OF HIS SERVICE ARE ALL OUTLINED IN MY REPORT, WHICH I ASSUME YOU'VE READ.

BITNER REPORTS THAT, DESPITE HIS BEST EFFORTS, ROBOT 44 CANNOT BE REVIVED AND HAS BEEN DECOMMISSIONED.

THOUGH THE ROBOT SECURITY FORCE IS FLAWED, ONE ROBOT SHOWED THAT HE WAS NOT JUST A PILE OF CIRCUIT BOARDS AND MOTORS, BUT A TRUE GALACTIC SECURITY AGENT.

BECAUSE OF VALOR PROVEN IN THE FIELD AND THE ULTIMATE SACRIFICE PAID, I PROPOSE THAT ROBOT 44 RECEIVE THE HONORARY TITLE OF GALACTIC FIELD AGENT.

THE COUNCIL HAS CONCLUDED TO ISSUE AN OFFICIAL NOTE OF GRATITUDE FOR ROBOT 44'S SERVICE.

HOWEVER, ULTIMATELY HE WAS JUST A TOOL, AN AID IN THE WORK DONE BY THE GALACTIC SECURITY AGENCY, AND AS SUCH IS DENIED AGENT STATUS.

THANK YOU, AGENT MISSILE MOUSE, YOU ARE DISMISSED.

AGENT MISSILE MOUSE!
WHAT'S GOING ON??

I AM ROBOT 358, SIR. I HAVE AN URGENT MESSAGE FROM CHIEF MAXWELL.

MM, WE'VE BEEN LOOKING ALL OVER FOR YOU...

WE'VE GOT A HOSTAGE SITUATION AT OUR EMBASSY ON CORBOTH 3. NEGOTIATIONS HAVE FAILED, SO WE NEED SOMEONE TO GET THE JOB DONE.

GOT IT, MAXWELL, BUT I'LL NEED A BACKUP SQUADRON OF SECURITY BOTS.

WAIT, YOU *WANT* TO WORK WITH BOTS?

JUST GET THEM BEFORE I CHANGE MY MIND.

YOU GOT IT, MM.

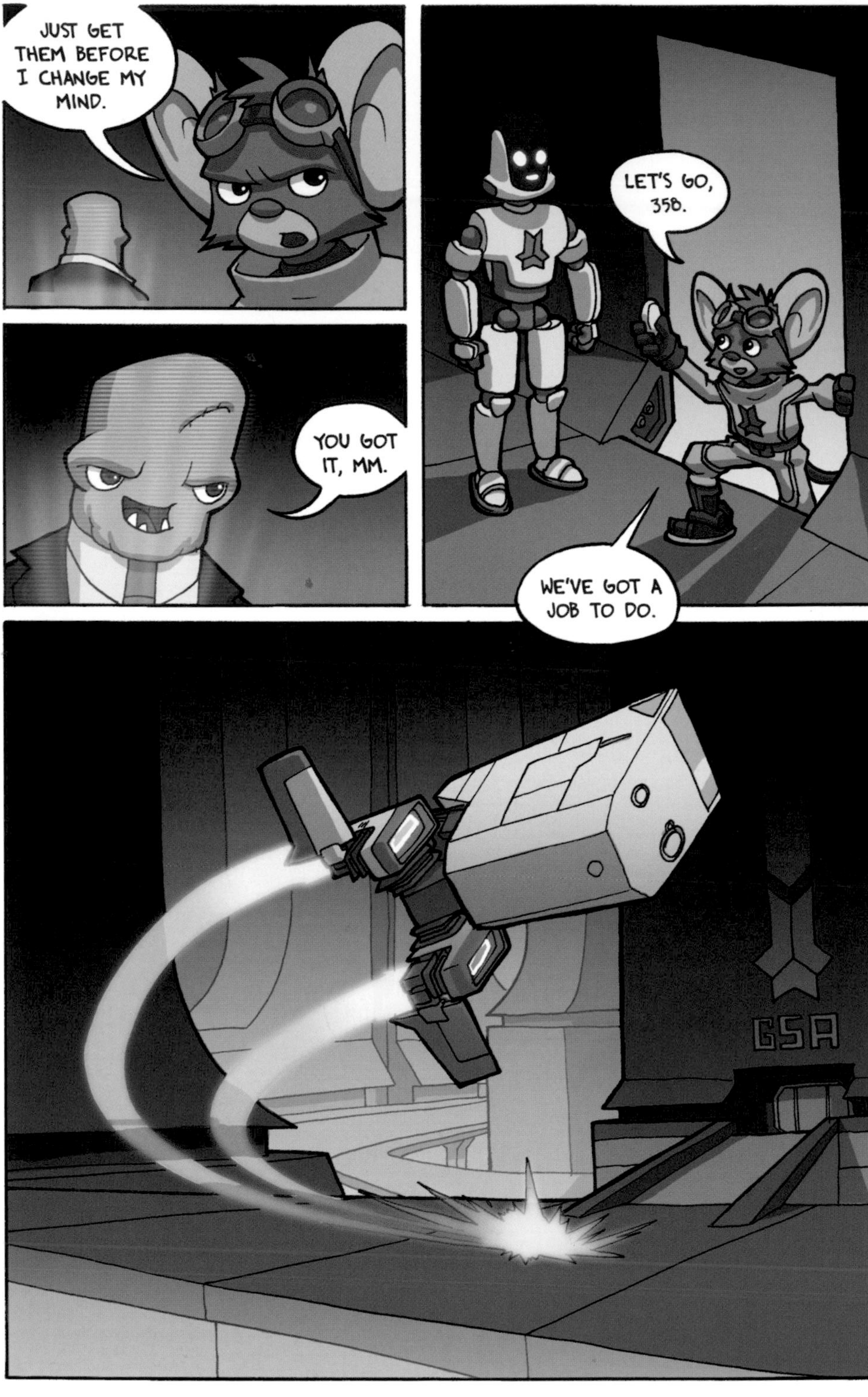

LET'S GO, 358.
WE'VE GOT A JOB TO DO.

GSA

THE GSA ARCHIVAL CENTER.
HEY, RON, WHATCHA GOT TODAY?
JUST DROPPING OFF A BUSTED SECURITY BOT.
ALL RIGHT, SIGN HERE.

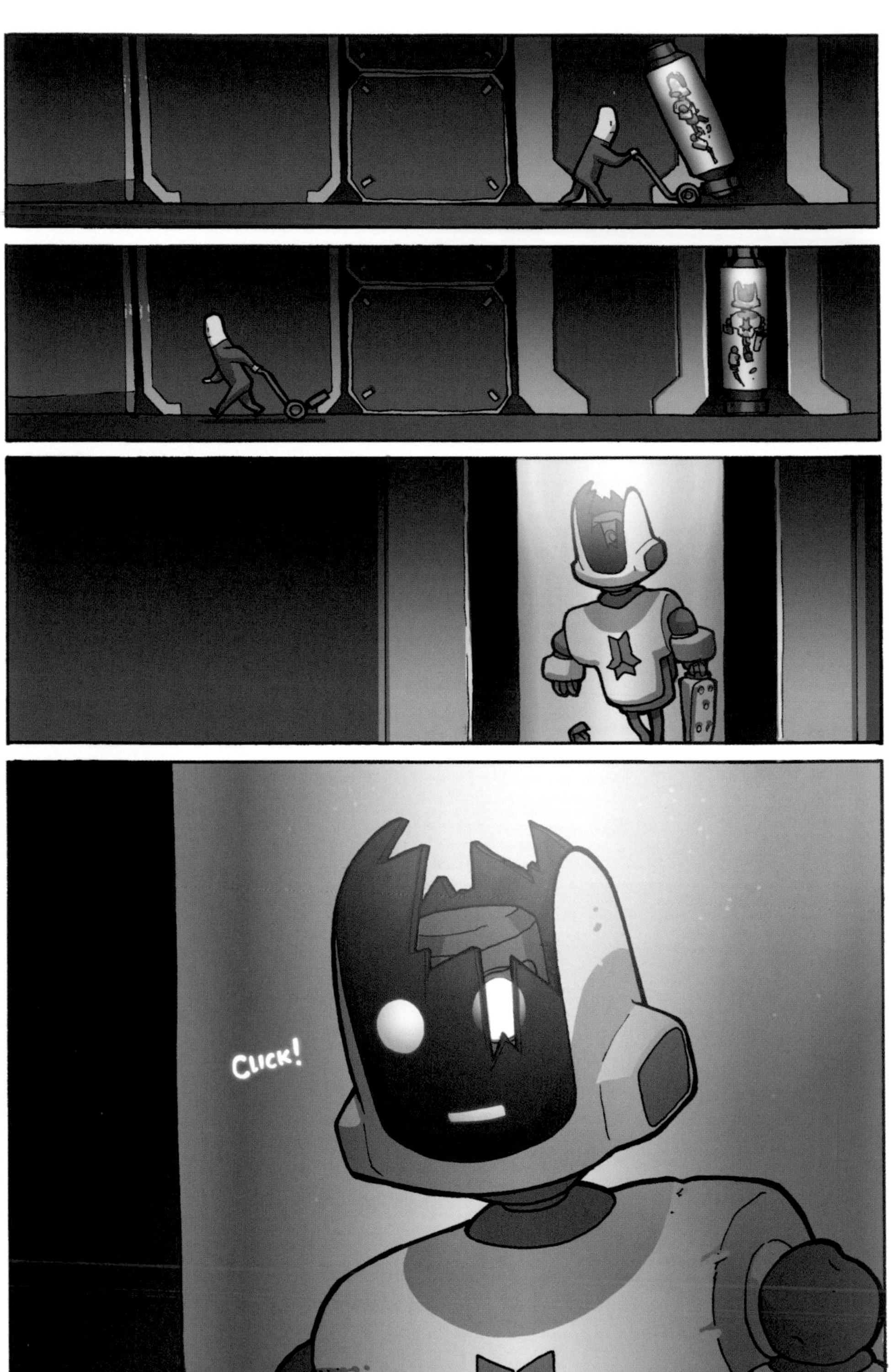
CLICK!

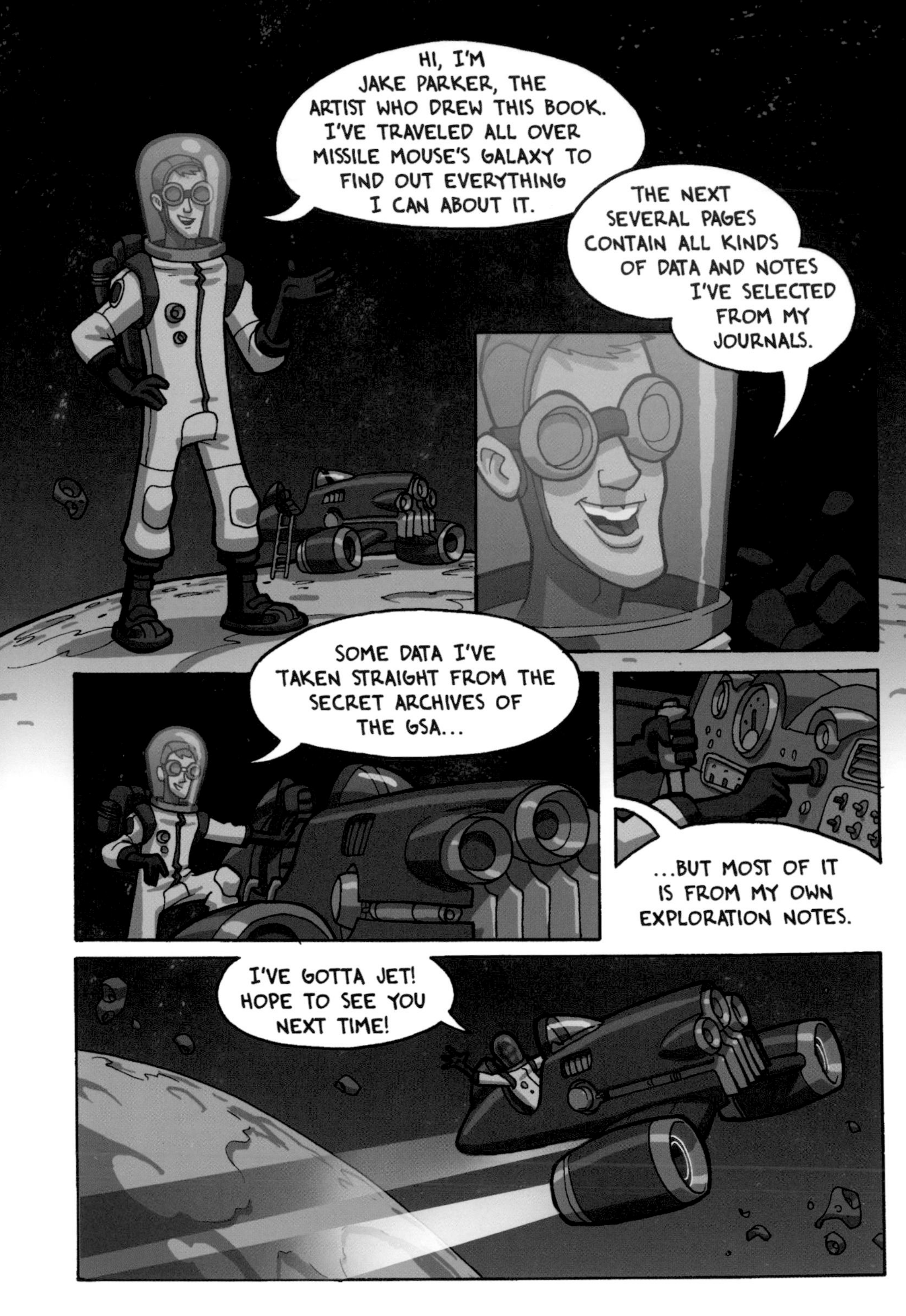
HI, I'M JAKE PARKER, THE ARTIST WHO DREW THIS BOOK. I'VE TRAVELED ALL OVER MISSILE MOUSE'S GALAXY TO FIND OUT EVERYTHING I CAN ABOUT IT.
THE NEXT SEVERAL PAGES CONTAIN ALL KINDS OF DATA AND NOTES I'VE SELECTED FROM MY JOURNALS.
SOME DATA I'VE TAKEN STRAIGHT FROM THE SECRET ARCHIVES OF THE GSA...
...BUT MOST OF IT IS FROM MY OWN EXPLORATION NOTES.
I'VE GOTTA JET! HOPE TO SEE YOU NEXT TIME!

MISSILE MOUSE
GUIDE TO THE UNIVERSE

MISSILE MOUSE is an agent for the Galactic Security Agency. He is an expert pilot and a crack shot. What he lacks in finesse he makes up for in dogged determination. Just when the GSA thinks he's too much of a liability, he proves them wrong and becomes an asset they can't function without.

He is a native Rodentian, but he does not remember his home world. Dire circumstances forced his father to escape the planet in secret with baby M and relocate to an asteroid belt in a nearby system. When tragedy struck and his father was killed, M joined the GSA and became known as Missile Mouse.

MM wears a standard GSA flight suit. His ArmorFlex™ undergarment is blaster and blade resistant, waterproof, and chemical proof. The outer suit provides thermal insulation, shielding from solar radiation, and protection from micrometeoroids and other space debris. MM sports the GSA elite rank colors of gold and red, indicating that he is a solo agent.

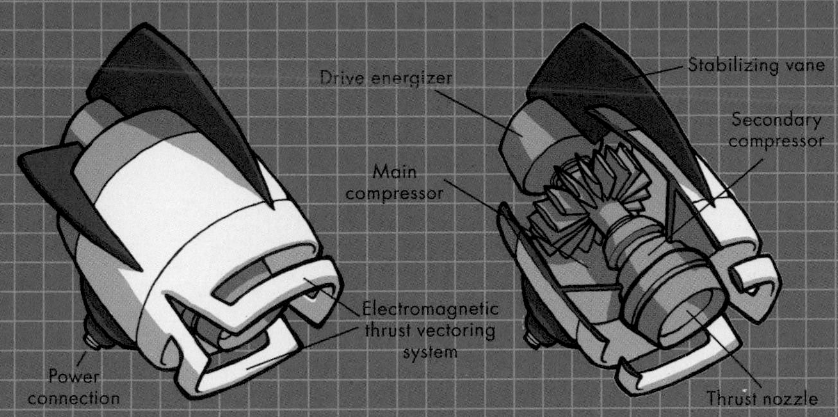

JET PACK

One of the few agents with enough coordination to pilot a jet pack, Missile Mouse prefers the UberTech™ RS600. Its compact size and extremely quiet operation perfectly fit his needs. He pilots the jet pack using control devices worn around each ankle.

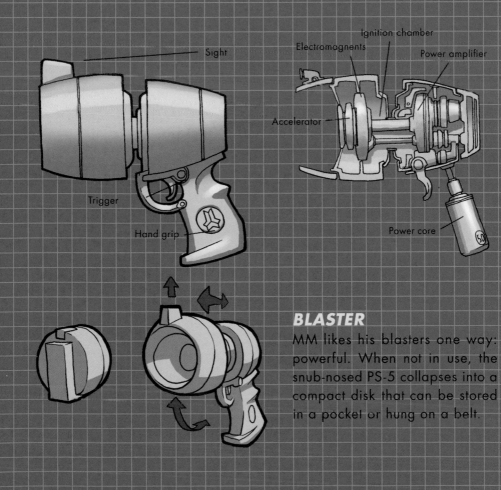

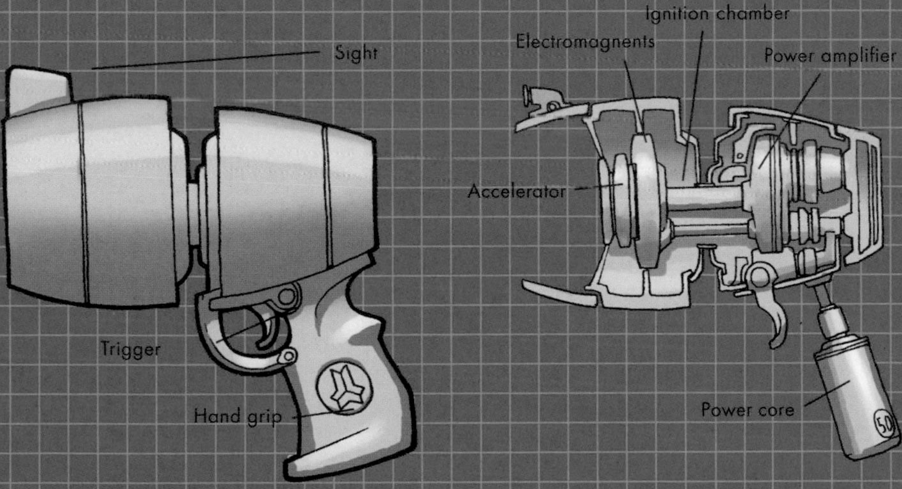

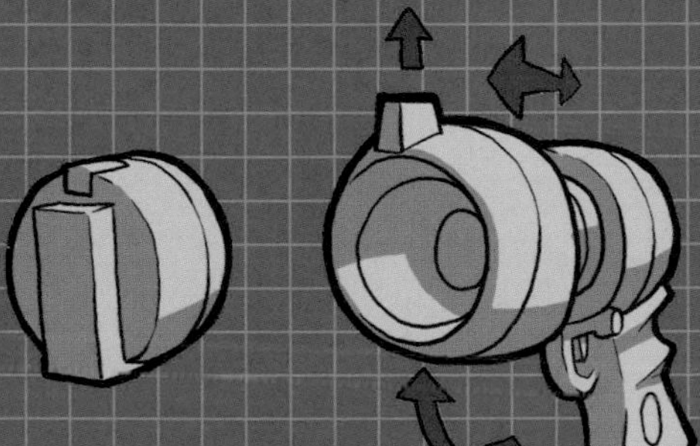

Sight
Trigger
Hand grip
Ignition chamber
Electromagnents
Power amplifier
Accelerator
Power core

BLASTER

MM likes his blasters one way: powerful. When not in use, the snub-nosed PS-5 collapses into a compact disk that can be stored in a pocket or hung on a belt.

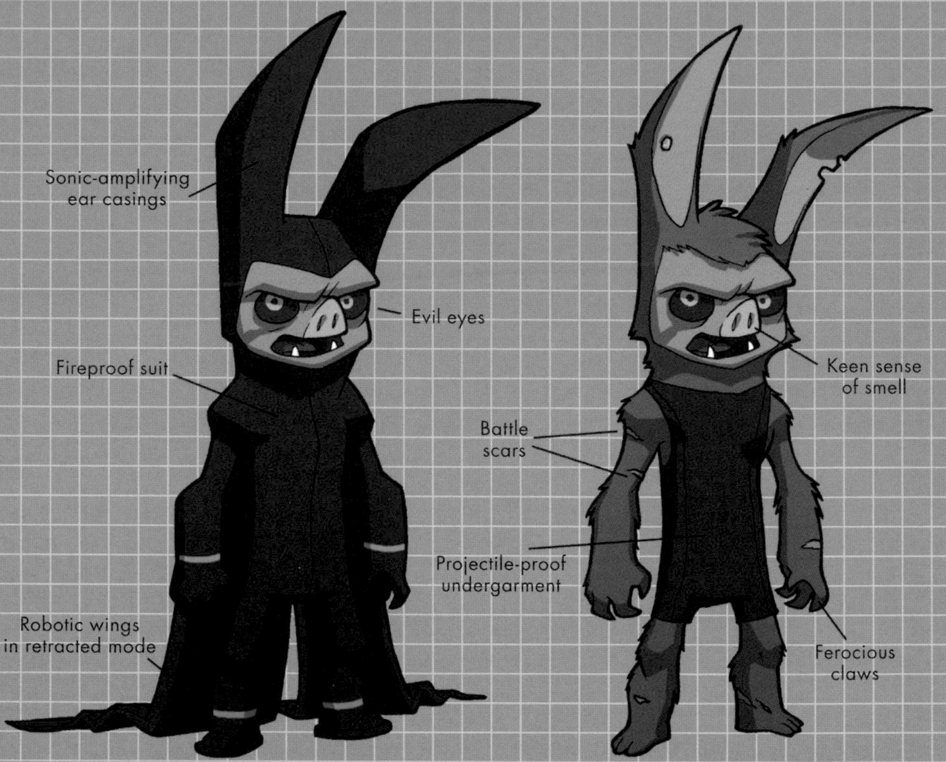

Sonic-amplifying ear casings

Evil eyes

Fireproof suit

Robotic wings in retracted mode

Keen sense of smell

Battle scars

Projectile-proof undergarment

Ferocious claws

BLAZING BAT is an intergalactic bounty hunter. His origins are clouded in mystery, but his reputation as a calculating and efficient hunter is known throughout the galactic underground. With his custom-made flamethrower, he is a lethal force not to be trifled with. Blazing Bat has taken on assignments that have pushed the limits of his unique capabilities, as his many scars can attest. One job early in his career ended badly and caused him to lose his wings. Undeterred, the tenacious bounty hunter developed a pair of robotic wings faster and more powerful than his original wings, making him even more formidable.

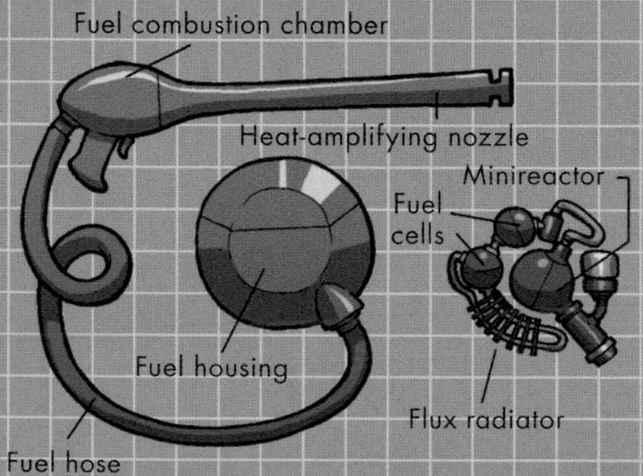

FLAMETHROWER

Blazing Bat's custom weapon utilizes advanced hyperfuels – allowing it to cut through any material with ease. Its primary purpose is less known and more sinster: intimidating his prey.

ROBO-WING TECHNOLOGY

Blazing Bat prefers maneuverability over flat-out speed. He had this function in mind when he lost his own wings and replaced them with powerful custom-made robo-wings rather than with a common jet pack. The skeleton wings retract and compact themselves into a tight cluster on the wing harness when not in use.

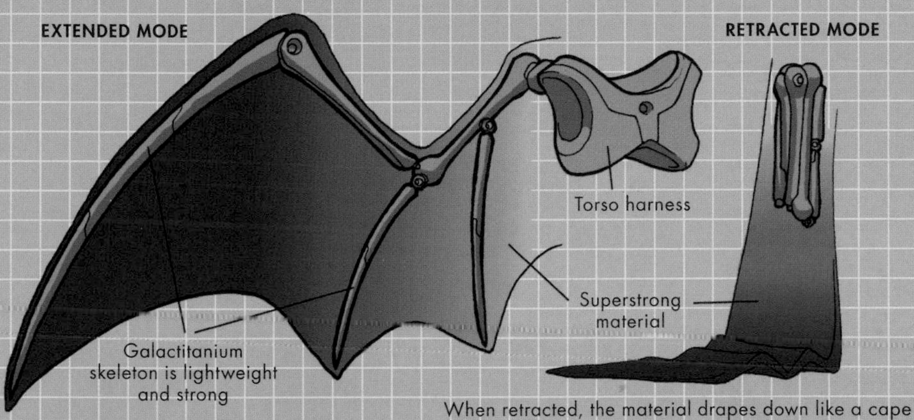

BLAZING BAT'S SHIP

Blazing Bat flies a retrofitted Gorgonian Space Fleet fighter. The unique cockpit allows for impressive 360° visibility, a crucial advantage in dangerous situations. Blazing Bat replaced a rear gunner cockpit with cargo space and installed powerful Snake-Cords for detaining his targets.

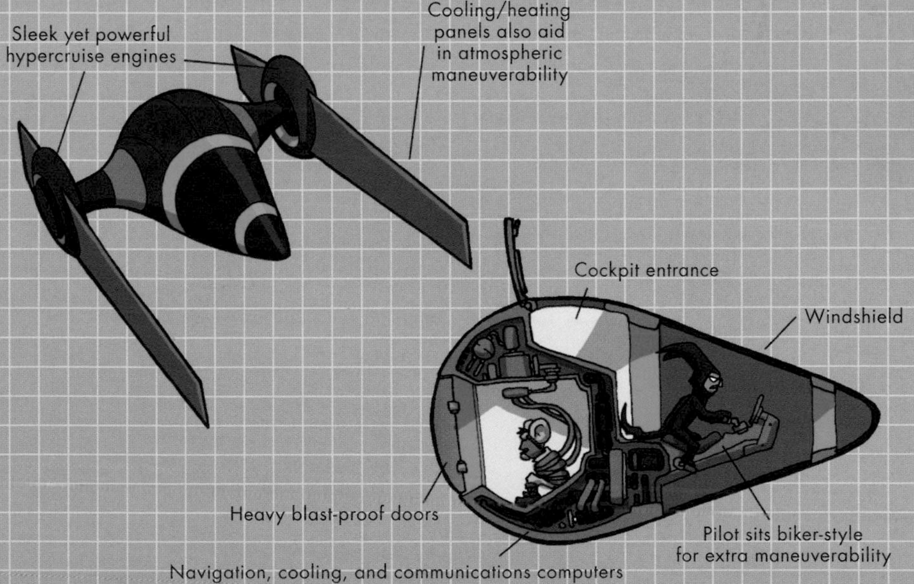

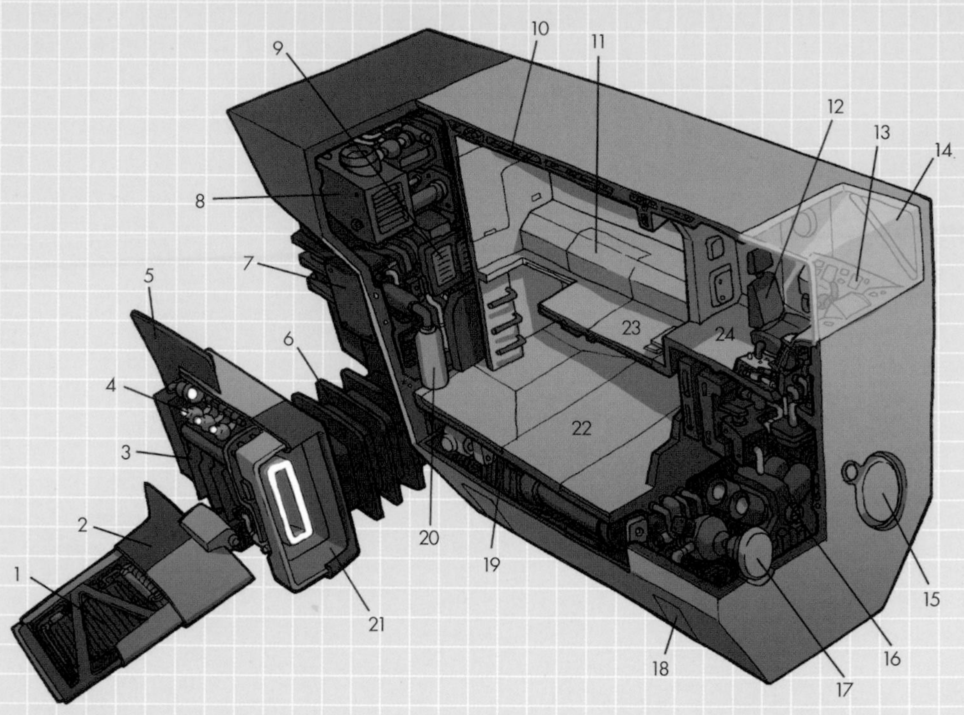

YA-33 FOXRUNNER is a formidable ship, despite its boxy appearance. It is a twin-ion-engine intergalactic utility vessel designed to perform an array of missions, including tactical transport of galactic agents, evacuations, and intergalactic transport. It can be customized depending on the needs of the mission and is a valuable asset to the GSA. One variation includes a much larger front-loading version capable of carrying an entire team of security bots.

1. Radiator panel
2. Durable astrotanium plating
3. Retrothruster accelerators
4. Ionic capacitors
5. Electromagnetic vector vane
6. Cooling vanes
7. External flux drive
8. Internal energy router
9. Main-stage reactor
10. Internal wiring
11. Personnel cargo space
12. Pilot's seat
13. Main controls
14. Transparent astrotanium windshield
15. Active scanner module
16. Communcations processor
17. Long-wave sensor array
18. Landing pad
19. Internal landing gear components
20. Fuel cell
21. Thruster intake
22. Main cargo space
23. Personnel space
24. Cockpit

ROBOT 44, GALACTIC SECURITY SUPPORT BOT

When the Galactic Security Agency found itself short on security agents, they turned to robotics. An elite team of scientists, field agents, engineers, and programmers developed the Galactic Security Support Bot to alleviate some of the pressure on the security agents. Robot 44 is considered one of the successes of this program. Where other bots faltered, 44 rose to the occasion and proved capable of handling anything assigned to him.

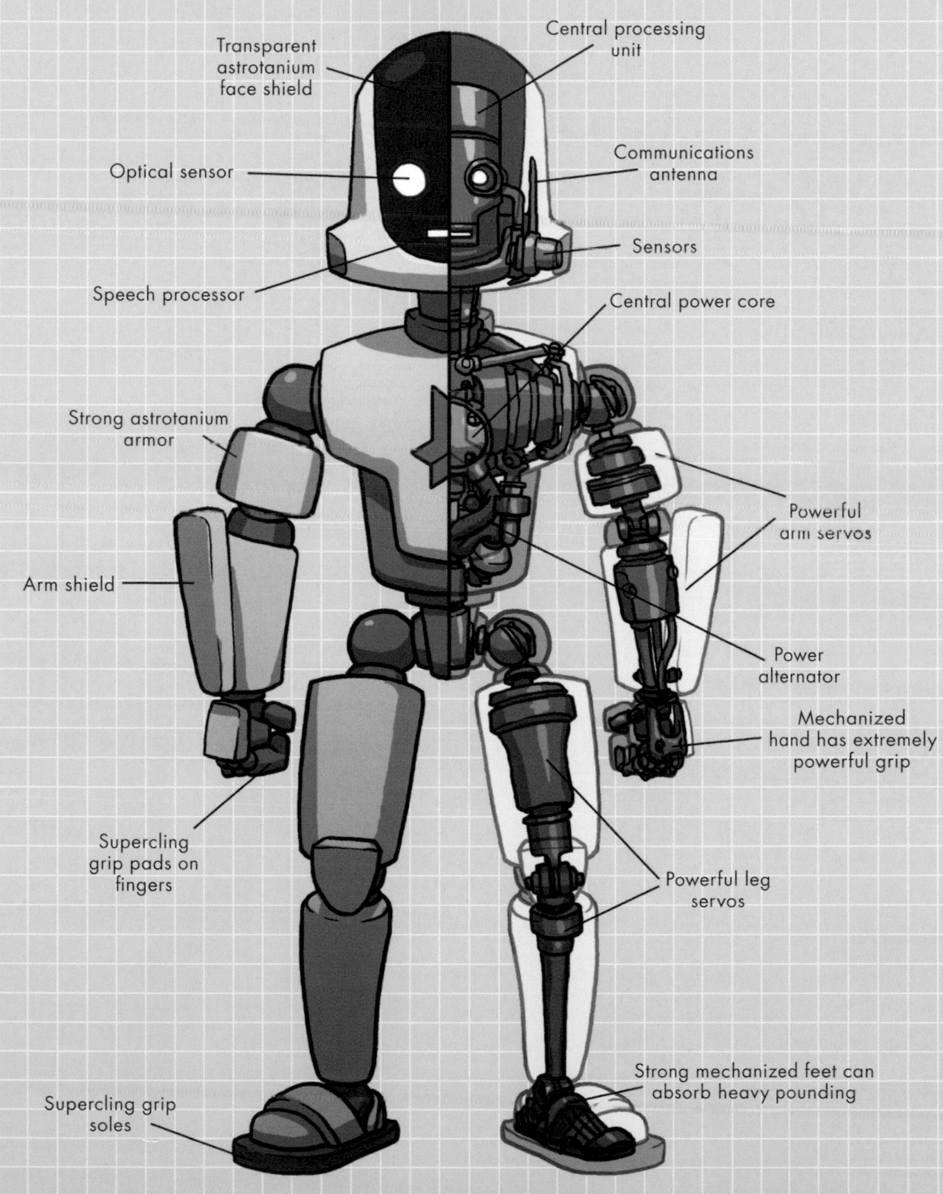

LASUKUS, TANKIAN FLIGHTKEEPER

Lasukus is a member of the predominant sapient species on the planet Tankium3. Never far from water, the Tankians built a mighty fortress city surrounded by flooded grain fields. These fields are harvested twice a year and the grain is stored in silos around the city. Every Tankian has a specific job to do for the community. Lasukus is the latest in a long line of Flightkeepers. Flights are flying reptiles that the Tankians use for scouting missions. Lasukus learned to keep flights from his father and will pass this skill on to his children when they are old enough to fly.

TANKIAN GROWTH CYCLE

1. The first year of a Tankian's life is spent under water as a small fertilized egg.

2. The egg hatches and a tadpole emerges.

3. Soon legs have grown and the gills are fully functioning.

4. With all limbs fully developed and gills suited for both water and air, the Tankian can now survive on land.

5. After about 3 years, the tail begins to shrink. The Tankian becomes bipedal and learns to speak.

6. By the time the Tankian is 12, the tail is completely gone.

7. Roughly five feet tall with slender yet powerful muscles, the Tankian is now matured.

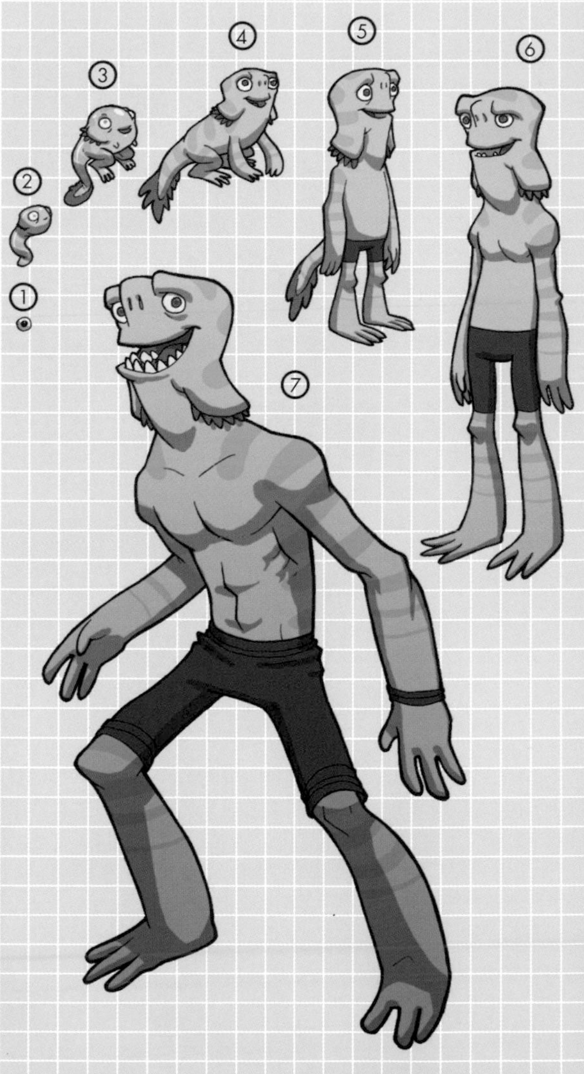

A TANKIUM HOME

Tankian family units are very important to the society's strength. More than just a shelter from the elements, the home is a central hub for the family, a refuge in case of emergencies, and a symbol of unity. Each home is self-sustaining, utilizing large water reservoirs in the basement to grow food for the family. Tankian homes are usually multiple stories tall, to save space in the walled city.

Jake Parker was born in Mesa, Arizona, and raised on a healthy diet of cereal, comic books, and Saturday morning cartoons. Now he draws comic books, works on animated films, and still eats lots of cereal. He's also done artwork for commercials, video games, kids' TV shows, and even a dinosaur exhibit for a museum. He currently lives in Provo, Utah, with his wife and five children.

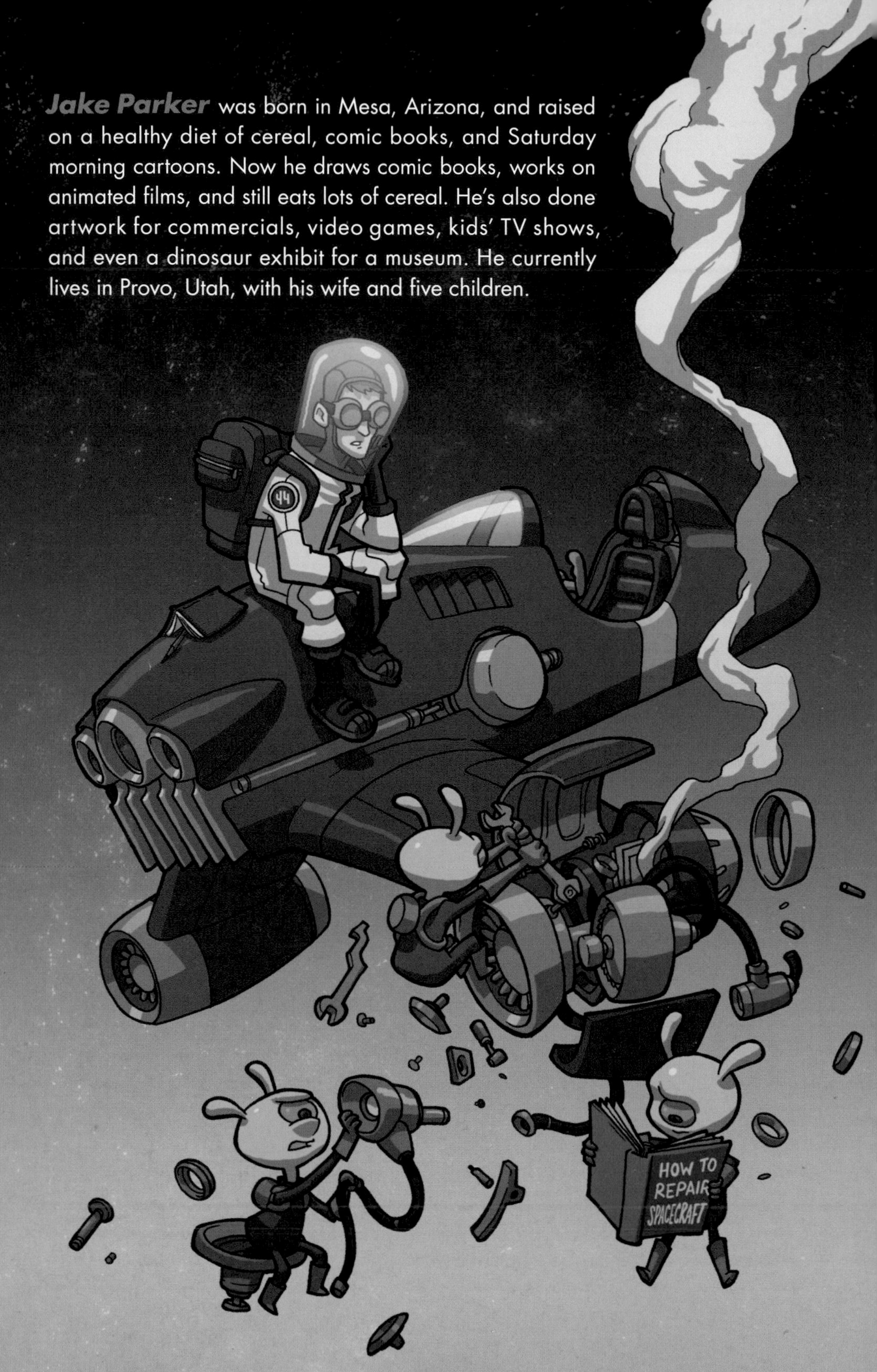